"Who are you and what are you doing here?"

"I'm Lina. I'm here to serve you." Her gaze skittered away. She swallowed, the movement accentuating her long, slender throat and the beauty of her pale gold skin.

For a dazed second Sayid's brain snared on the idea of nuzzling her fragrant flesh. He caught the scent of roses on her skin and wondered how she'd taste.

The temptation was so alluring, he stepped back to be sure he didn't act on it.

"Who sent you?"

"My father's brother. He sent me as a goodwill gift to the previous emir."

A goodwill gift! Sourness filled Sayid's mouth. That was the sort of nation his uncle had ruled. Where a woman could be treated as a commodity. As the new emir, he had a lot of work to bring the country into the current century.

"The previous emir is dead. You are free to go. You're not required here."

"I can't leave, sir." She curved her lips in a tentative smile that didn't show in her eyes. "I now belong to you."

Growing up near the beach, **Annie West** spent lots of time observing tall, burnished lifeguards—early research! Now she spends her days fantasizing about gorgeous men and their love lives. Annie has been a reader all her life. She also loves travel, long walks, good company and great food. You can contact her at annie@annie-west.com or via PO Box 1041, Warners Bay, NSW 2282, Australia.

Books by Annie West

Harlequin Presents

The Flaw in Raffaele's Revenge
Seducing His Enemy's Daughter

One Night With Consequences

Contracted for the Petrakis Heir
A Vow to Secure His Legacy

The Princess Seductions

His Majesty's Temporary Bride
The Greek's Forbidden Princess

Wedlocked!

The Desert King's Captive Bride

Secret Heirs of Billionaires

The Desert King's Secret Heir

Visit the Author Profile page
at Harlequin.com for more titles.

Annie West

———

INHERITED FOR THE
ROYAL BED

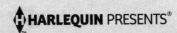

Recycling programs
for this product may
not exist in your area.

ISBN-13: 978-1-335-41951-4

Inherited for the Royal Bed

First North American publication 2018

Copyright © 2018 by Annie West

For questions and comments about the quality of this book, please contact us at CustomerService@Harlequin.com.

Printed in U.S.A.

www.Harlequin.com

INHERITED FOR THE ROYAL BED

This one is for you, Grace Thiele:
your very own sheikh story.

I love your unbounded enthusiasm for my sheikhs,
which makes me want to write more.

And a huge thank-you to Ana Neves for your
language assistance.

You're a gem!

CHAPTER ONE

THREE MEN STRODE through the gleaming marble corridors of the Emir's palace.

Past the great council room where the walls were hung with decorative displays of lances, swords and ancient muskets. Where brightly coloured martial standards hung as if waiting for the next call to arms.

Past sumptuous banqueting halls and audience chambers. Past colonnaded courtyards filled with pleasure gardens, the tinkle of fountains loud in this still hour after midnight. The only other noise was the march of boots.

Past the studded medieval door to the empty harem and another that led to the passage carved down, through the very rock of the citadel, to the vast treasure chambers and dungeons.

Finally they reached the corridor to the Emir's private suite.

Sayid paused. 'That will be all for now.'

'But, sire, our orders are—'

Sayid swung round. 'Your orders change tonight. Halarq is no longer on the brink of war.'

Saying it aloud still sounded unreal. Halarq had been on the verge of war most of his life, principally, but not solely, with the neighbouring kingdom of Jeirut. It was why every male was armed and trained to defend his country to the death.

Sayid thought of all those years primed for conflict. Of unending border skirmishes and casualties. Of missed opportunities to invest in better lives for the people, as opposed to diverting energy and funds into armaments.

His mouth firmed. If he achieved nothing else, he, Sayid Badawi, the new Emir of Halarq, had done that—brought peace. Later, when it sank in, he'd rejoice. Tonight all he wanted was to lay his head on a pillow for the first time in three days and find oblivion.

'But, sire, our duty is to protect you. We spend the night at the guard stations outside your suite.' The soldier nodded towards the other end of the long arched corridor.

'The palace is guarded by your colleagues on the perimeter and by the latest security technology.' Sayid's uncle, the previous Emir, had spent lavishly on his own protection and comfort, as well as on armaments.

It was a shame he hadn't been as ready to spend on his people.

Still the guards didn't shift. Sayid's patience frayed. 'Those are my orders,' he barked. His eyes narrowed and the guard blanched.

Instantly Sayid's anger eased. The man was only trying to do his duty as he understood it. Questioning the orders of the Emir would, in the past, have met with terrible punishment.

'Your devotion to duty, and to your Emir, is noted and appreciated.' He surveyed both men, giving them time to absorb that. 'But our security arrangements are changing. Your commander will brief you on that later. In the meantime, it's my desire, and my order, that you return to the guard hall.' He didn't wait for a response but turned away.

'That will be all,' he said as he strode down the corridor, his dusty boots leaving marks on the graceful inlaid patterns underfoot.

Silence. They hadn't attempted to follow.

Sayid filled his lungs with the cool night air wafting from a nearby courtyard. This was the first time he'd been alone in days. The first time he could allow himself to relax.

Tonight's ebullient celebrations with every Halarqi clan leader, regional governor and warlord, plus most of their fighting men, had been on a monumental scale. The plain beyond the city walls was filled to the brim and the scents of festive cooking fires drifted through the whole city. Every so often the crackle of rifle fire indicated the celebration continued. They'd probably still be at it as dawn broke.

Whereas he'd be up at sunrise, in the office he hadn't had time to make his own since his uncle's death, immersed in the paperwork and diplomatic detail that would put flesh on the bones of the peace agreement. A peace that guaranteed the borders, the safe passage of travellers and even, potentially, trade and mutual development between Halarq and Jeirut.

Sayid's pace slowed and he smiled, the action tugging his cheek muscles taut.

Who could blame his people for celebrating? He'd do the same if he weren't weary from the long negotiations with Huseyn of Jeirut. And from keeping his more bellicose generals in check long enough to prevent provocation and violence. Some had thought, despite his military record and his reputation for decisive action, he'd be easily swayed into supporting his predecessor's war plans. But Sayid's priority was his people, not the posturing of old men who thought others' lives expendable.

Reaching the Emir's private suite, he entered, a sigh of relief escaping as the tall door closed behind him. Alone, finally.

Sayid strode through, past the study and the media room, through the vast sitting room and lavish private dining parlour, to the bedroom. His eyes went immediately to the vast, beckoning bed. Its cover, embroidered in the royal colours of blue and silver, was pulled back invitingly. The overhead light was off, leaving only the gentle glow of a few decorative pierced lamps.

He rocked to a halt, tempted to forget about the state of his clothes and just topple onto the mattress as he was. He'd be asleep within seconds.

Instead he crossed the spacious room towards the bathroom. He'd shower first.

Sayid pulled off his clothes as he walked, his tension easing as the hand-stitched layers came off. The fine cotton of his shirt masked a jaw-cracking yawn as he tugged it up, over his head, rolling his shoulders in appreciation as he felt cool night air brush his flesh.

He was about to toe off one boot when something made him pause. He stilled, his weight on one foot, his senses prickling at the certainty something was out of place.

A lifetime's training as a warrior, always aware, put him on alert.

Something was wrong. He was certain in less time than it took to form the thought.

It would serve him right if he'd dismissed his guard only to find himself under threat in his own chambers. The youngest and shortest-lived Emir of Halarq in all its history. That would be a fine epitaph!

Keeping his movements easy, Sayid wrapped the cotton of his discarded shirt around his left hand and forearm. The cloth wouldn't stop a bullet but might deflect a knife in a pinch. He didn't spare a glance for the long silvered scar running up that arm from his wrist to well past his elbow. It proved a well-honed knife could easily cut through several layers of clothing.

Slowly he turned, nostrils flared to capture any unusual scent, eyes narrowing as he peered into the darkened corners of the room.

Nothing. Exhaustion must be interfering with his perception.

Sayid swung right around towards the bed again and—

He stiffened, his hand going to the ceremonial but razor-sharp dagger at his hip.

'Who are you?' The words issued through clenched teeth. 'What are you doing here?'

As he spoke the figure in the dark corner beyond the bed rose. A small figure, its outline blurred by a swathe of fabric wrapped around its shoulders and over its head.

Having risen, the person immediately bowed low in a silent gesture of obeisance.

Sayid's senses screamed a warning. What would have happened if he hadn't noticed that still, silent figure hiding in the corner? Would they have waited till his back was turned in the shower, or he was fast asleep, to slip a knife between his ribs?

Had he been foolish to write off his dead uncle's preoccupation with security? The man had been dangerously paranoid and increasingly erratic but he'd been wily.

'Come here!'

Instantly the figure glided closer.

'Sire.' A soft, whispery voice feathered his skin like a lover's caress. Another bow. This time when the figure straightened, it tugged off the enveloping blanket.

Sayid stared.

His privacy had been invaded by a dancing girl? He shook his head. Did weariness play tricks with his vision?

Women in his country didn't dress like this. Women in Halarq dressed modestly. Some covered their hair but all covered their bodies.

This one didn't.

Heat speared his belly and drilled into his groin as he surveyed her. She wore a low-slung skirt that fell in gauzy folds from the curve of her hips. He clearly saw long slim legs through the fabric. She shifted and a glimpse of toned, honey-coloured thigh appeared through a slit in the skirt.

His gaze rose to a bare midriff, deliciously curved into a tiny waist, then up to a cropped, sleeveless top of shiny material that clasped her like a second skin. It was cut low, showing off the upper slopes of enticing breasts that rose and fell with her rapid breathing.

Sayid's throat closed as if he'd gulped down half the eastern desert. His fingers stretched then curled into fists, bunching at his sides.

Competing impulses warred.

To command she cover herself instantly.

But that wasn't his first reaction.

To reach out and touch that inviting body.

Yes. That.

To haul her against him and revel in the pleasure a woman's soft body could afford a man wearied by days, no, weeks of achieving the impossible—first keeping his uncle from invading Jeirut, then, on his uncle's death, finding a way to ensure a lasting peace between nations that were traditional enemies.

His gaze rose further, taking in a face of extraordinary loveliness. Dark hair, unbound, was pushed behind her shoulders. Her breasts, pert and high, rose shakily with each breath.

Imagination told him her skin would be warm silk, soft and pleasurable.

Sayid, like his uncle before him, was a man of strong desires, with a predilection for pleasure. Yet, unlike his dead uncle, Sayid prided himself on ruling his sensual side. He'd seen what unbridled self-indulgence did to a man. He had no intention of following his uncle down that path. Instead he emulated his father who'd been a warrior prince, bound by an unshakeable code of conduct. A man who channelled strong appetites into a drive to protect and serve his people.

'Look at me.' The command was overloud. But Sayid's control over his body was sorely tried.

Instantly her bowed head tilted up.

Sayid registered another unseen body blow. This time to his solar plexus. For her eyes were unlike any he'd seen. They were the colour of wild violets in the mountains. Darker than blue, softer than purple.

He scowled. Not only was she remarkably pretty, she was young—too young to be alone in his room.

'Who are you?'

'Lina, sire.' Again that low bow, which now, to his horror, made his groin grow tight and hard, for he got an eyeful as she bent forward. It looked as if her breasts might pop free of her top at any moment.

'Don't do that!'

She blinked, emotion he couldn't read flashing across her features. Then it disappeared as she lifted her chin to look somewhere near his shoulder, her hands clasped neatly before her. 'Do what, sire?'

'Bowing. Don't do it again.'

Her brow furrowed. 'But sire! You are the Emir. It wouldn't be seemly—'

'Let me be the judge of seemly.' Sayid raised a hand to the back of his neck, rubbing at too-tight muscles.

'Yes, sire.' Yet her brow twitched as if in disagreement and he'd swear she bit her lip as if to stop herself saying more.

'Don't call me that, either.' His uncle might have enjoyed constant reminders of his status as ruler of the nation, but Sayid had heard the title too often from too many toadying courtiers trying to ingratiate themselves. It grated.

He'd give a lot to talk with someone who didn't bow and scrape. He scrubbed a hand over his face, knowing fatigue shortened his temper.

His mouth kicked up at the memory of his tense negotiations this week with Huseyn of Jeirut, the man known as the Iron Hand. There'd been no bowing and scraping then. The man was the toughest negotiator Sayid had met, as well as a formidable warrior. Yet, despite the weight of responsibility on their shoulders as they worked towards a peace deal for their nations, Sayid had enjoyed the stimulation of dealing with the man.

Halarq, under the rule of Sayid's uncle, hadn't been a place where people spoke their mind. The palace was full of advisers trained to agree with their Emir, rather than advise without fear or favour.

Yet another thing Sayid aimed to change.

'As you wish…sir.'

He opened his mouth then shut it. 'Sir' was marginally better than 'sire'. What did it matter anyway? He was so tired he'd allowed himself to be distracted.

'Who are you and what are you doing here?'

'I'm Lina. I'm here to serve you—' her gaze skittered away to fix on a point beyond him '—in any way you wish.' She swallowed, the movement accentuating her long slender throat and the beauty of her pale gold skin.

For a dazed second Sayid's brain snared on the idea of nuzzling her fragrant flesh. He caught the scent of roses on her skin and wondered how she'd taste.

The temptation was so alluring, he stepped back to be sure he didn't act on it. She stiffened at his movement, revealing a tension she fought to hide.

'Who sent you?'

'My father's brother. He sent me as a goodwill gift to the previous Emir.'

A goodwill gift! Sourness filled Sayid's mouth. That was the sort of nation his uncle had ruled. Where a woman could be treated as a commodity. Old memories stirred, leaving a rancid taste on his tongue.

As the new Emir, he had a lot of work to bring the country into the current century.

'The previous Emir is dead.'

Sayid had believed the women in his uncle's harem had been sent away as the old man's prostate illness worsened and he became impotent.

'I know, s…sir. He died soon after my arrival and I never met him.' Her eyes flickered to his, then away. 'My condolences on your loss.'

'Thank you.' Sayid felt neither loss nor sorrow at his uncle's death. The old man had been a poor steward for their country and personally deplorable, a mean, brutal voluptuary. 'But with his death, you are free to go. You're not required here.'

Huge violet eyes met his. Was that fear he read there? 'Oh, no. You misunderstand. That is—' she swallowed, dropping her gaze to the floor as if afraid she'd said the wrong thing '—not *misunderstand*, of course.'

She shook her head and a lock of glossy dark hair slid over her shoulder, curling past her breast all the way to her waist. For the life of him, Sayid couldn't tear his gaze from it.

'I can't leave, sir. It's all been arranged.' She curved her lips in a tentative smile that didn't show in her eyes. 'With your uncle's death I now belong to you.'

CHAPTER TWO

IF LINA HAD thought Sayid Badawi had looked stern before, he was positively thunderous now. His brow scrunched in a furrow of disapproval and his honed jaw clenched as if biting back an oath.

Yet the gleam of those dark eyes and the sudden flare of his nostrils spoke of something more intimate than fury.

Masculine awareness.

Lina knew something about that. She'd witnessed the way men had reacted to her mother's beauty. And since Lina herself had reached puberty she'd seen a similar look from the men who'd occasionally visited her home.

She swallowed hard.

Not her home now. Her uncle's home.

Yet unlike her male cousins, who didn't just look but who tried to touch, the Emir kept his hands to himself.

Lina dropped her gaze, as she'd been taught. But without the magnetic draw of those dark, glittering eyes to distract her, she became far too aware of the rest of him.

A long, lean body that tapered from straight shoulders down via an intriguing display of bronzed skin and taut muscle to narrow hips that thankfully were still covered in pale trousers. Nor could she help but notice the muscled strength of his thighs. A rider's thighs. The only thing marring the perfection of his toned form was a pale scar extending down one arm.

Lina didn't know whether to blame the shock of finally being alone with the man who was to be her master, or her first sight of a half-naked man. Or perhaps his stunning attractiveness. But she felt lightheaded. Her breathing came too fast and her thoughts scrambled.

She'd arrived at the palace expecting to be at the beck and call of a much older man, renowned for his short temper and unforgiving nature. Instead she found herself bequeathed to a man in his mid-twenties whose looks would make any woman sigh. He was fit and handsome. But more, there was an inner strength about him and a quality she couldn't name, yet read in his proud face with its heavy-lidded eyes, strong nose and square, solid jaw.

Whatever it was, it made sensation fizz and burst through her veins. Was she ill? Coming down with a fever? She'd never felt like this before.

'Lina?'

She darted a look at his face. Clearly he'd spoken and she hadn't responded. A chill clamped the back of her neck and skittered all the way down her spine. Was his temper as volatile as the old Emir's? Her aunt had told hair-raising tales of what awaited if she didn't do exactly as commanded by her royal master, no matter how difficult or…unfamiliar.

'Sir?'

'I said you are not needed here. You can return to your home.'

Lina blinked, her eyes widening in dismay. She'd been horrified by the whispered gossip about what the previous Emir would expect her to do for him. Had wondered if some of the suggestions were even physically possible. But to be dismissed from the palace! That held its own terrors.

She swallowed, pain slicing as if her throat closed around a sharpened blade.

'Please, sir. I can't.'

Belatedly she lowered her gaze, knowing it was her place to obey, not argue. Her uncle and aunt had warned time after time that she must learn humility and silence. They'd made it their business to try turning her into a mute, obedient damsel. They would be horrified if they could hear her.

'You can if I tell you.' The Emir's tone was brusque, allowing no room for argument.

Lina felt herself stiffen as the enormity of her situation hit her. The freedom he offered, no, *commanded* she take, was an illusion.

She was utterly alone, with nowhere in the world to call home and no one who cared for her. She had no rights, no call on his compassion. She was nothing to him, or to anyone else.

Everything she'd been taught told her to nod, to back away and make herself scarce, for it wouldn't do to disobey the man who held her fate, even after he'd washed his hands of her.

He shifted and she sensed his impatience for her to be gone.

Yet Lina knew once she left this room she'd never

be allowed to enter again. Once out of the palace she'd be on the street, literally, with no resources, no friends and not even a scrap of respectable clothing.

She shuddered, imagining what would become of her.

Clasping her hands before her, willing them not to shake, she took a fortifying breath, which reminded her of the hated clothes she wore as her breasts swelled against the low-cut top.

'Sir.' She swallowed and lifted her chin. The Emir had already begun to turn away. He'd dismissed her and that meant she must go.

Except Lina couldn't.

'Well?' Ebony brows angled down above that imperious nose and his dark-shadowed jaw was set at an angle that warned his hold on patience was precarious.

She tilted her face higher, meeting his narrowed gaze. 'I have no home to go to, sir. Not any more. Or any family.' She bit her lip, refusing to let it tremble. 'Could I be allowed to remain in the palace? I'm a hard worker. I can make myself useful at any task. In the kitchens, the laundries, the...' She paused, racking her brain, wondering what the multitude of royal servants did all day. 'I can sew and embroider too.' Not well enough, as her aunt was fond of reminding her. But then she didn't do anything well enough for her aunt.

'You must have a home. Where did you come from?' No softening in the austere masculine beauty of that sculpted face. But at least he'd paused to listen. Her heart throbbed a hopeful beat.

'From the home of my father's brother, sir. But that door is no longer open to me.' It took everything Lina had to stand erect, meeting his gaze headlong, when harsh memories bombarded her. Of becoming little more than a slave in her own home.

The Emir sighed and lifted his hand to rake his fingers through his short hair. Intriguingly, the movement made muscles swell and tug in his arm, shoulder and chest. Lina had never before realised that such a simple movement could be so spellbinding.

But then she'd never seen a man like the Emir, naked or clothed.

He sighed and turned away. Abruptly her straying thoughts focused sharply. He was walking away, leaving her to her fate. Fear and despair vied with indignation. Lina was sick of fate, in the form of the men who had ruled her destiny, ignoring her.

Yet instead of continuing to the bathroom, he merely flung open a wardrobe and withdrew a shirt.

'Here.' The white garment flew through the air towards her. 'Put that on and sit down.'

Lina's fingers tightened convulsively on soft white cotton. So finely woven it was translucent. Only the finest material for the leader of the nation.

'Go on.' He nodded at the garment in her hands, then turned towards the bed. For a second she thought he was going to sit there, till he abruptly changed direction and headed for an armchair, sinking onto it with a sigh.

Hurriedly, Lina lifted the cotton over her head, pulling it down till it covered her almost to the knees. She had to roll up the sleeves to free her hands.

No doubt she looked like a child playing dress-up.

She puzzled over why the Emir thought the extra layer necessary. It was true, she was more comfortable with the bare skin of her waist and breasts covered, but from what she'd observed of men, they enjoyed such displays.

Unless the Emir wasn't interested in women?

The startling thought kept her rooted to the spot. Surely not! Such a waste that would be. Besides, there'd been that shimmer of heat when he'd looked at her before. It had been unmistakable.

She darted a curious glance at the man who would decide her future. He wasn't looking at her. In fact, he'd shut his eyes, which gave her time to take in more of his appearance, to see beyond that grave masculine beauty to the weariness bracketing his eyes and mouth. The slight droop of his head. The slump of that long frame in the cushioned chair.

The man was exhausted.

Sayid opened his eyes to see the girl dart into his bathroom. What the devil was she up to?

He was about to follow when she emerged, carrying a bowl of water. She sank to the floor before him in a show of fluid grace that made him wonder if she really was a dancer, as that scanty costume suggested.

Savagely he ignored the scorching trail of desire searing through his belly. He reminded himself he'd learned to master his impulsive, carnal nature.

Yet, to his chagrin the addition of his shirt did nothing to hide her allure. With fatigue testing both his patience and his willpower, it had seemed safest to cover her up so he couldn't see that too-inviting expanse of honey skin, the alluring dips, swells and hollows of her breasts, waist and hips.

Sayid hadn't reckoned on her being just as sexy, if

not more, wearing his shirt. Because it was *his* shirt? It conjured a sense of intimacy, as if she were a lover who'd already shared her body with him. The thought snagged in his brain, stirring heat in his groin.

The extra covering hinted at her shape, the fine fabric clinging here and there, teasing with what lay beneath.

'What are you doing?' His voice emerged brusque, making her jump, yet she didn't back away.

'Helping with your boots, sir.' She'd put the bowl to one side and reached forward as if to touch him, then halted, clearly waiting for permission.

'Look at me.' He was tired of the tradition that deterred people from daring to look their ruler in the face. Besides, it made it more difficult for him to read their thoughts.

Violet eyes met his. A burst of dark colour so deep it seemed Sayid could fall into it. Beautiful eyes, wide and slanted at the corners, giving her the look of a woman with secrets, or whose face was made for smiling.

There was no smile now. She still wore that tense expression, as if her flesh had shrunk around her bones, making her look wary, even scared, except the firm angle of her chin belied fear.

'How old are you?' The question wasn't the one he'd planned.

'Seventeen, sir.' She swallowed, then licked her bottom lip as if nervous.

A mere teenager. A judder of regret vibrated through him. Seventeen and scared despite her determination not to show it. While he was twenty-five and, right now, felt old beyond his years.

Sayid couldn't accept the invitation to let her *serve him in any way he wished*. Having a woman who'd been ordered to serve him was utterly unpalatable.

Or it *should* be.

Yet despite exhaustion part of him was disappointed. For Lina, with her pouting lips, her intriguing air of composure despite her nerves, and her outrageously luscious body, made the blood roar in his veins and heat stir. After all, he was descended from generations of marauding warriors, used to taking whatever they wanted, including women.

'May I help you with your boots, sir?'

'Very well.' If it helped her to feel useful, he wouldn't object. It would be tough getting her to speak if she were frozen into silence.

So he leaned back against the padded chair and stretched out one leg towards her, watching as she scooted closer, cradling the boot in her hands then drawing it off as carefully as if it were something precious and fragile.

Both boots, both socks were removed and set aside. Then she moved the bowl, lifted his legs one at a time and placed them in warm water.

Instantly Sayid felt some of the tension locking his muscles release.

'Thank you, Lina.' Her startled gaze told him she wasn't accustomed to thanks. 'Now, tell me about yourself.'

Again that flare of confusion in her stunning eyes. Whatever her story, she wasn't used to being asked about herself. She hesitated then moistened her lips with her tongue in a way that sent tension flicking through him like a whip.

'My name is Lina Rahman. My father was Head-man of Narjif.'

Sayid nodded. He knew the distant town and he'd met her father last year as he toured the provinces. A serious man and a traditionalist, set in his ways. But that didn't explain why he'd send his daughter as a gift to Sayid's uncle, a man notorious in his younger days for his womanising, and more lately, for his iras-cible temper.

'You have siblings?'

A dimple appeared in her cheek as if she bit it. 'Sadly no. My parents weren't blessed with sons, only me.' Clearly she repeated something she'd heard many times. Yet Sayid was pleased to see she met his gaze, not so shy now.

'He sent you to my uncle? To the old Emir?'

'No!' She shook her head and another long strand of dark hair slid over her shoulder to fall in a sinuous curve over her breast. 'My father is dead. It was his brother who sent me. He and his wife.'

Sayid frowned. 'And your mother?'

'She died years ago. If she'd been alive she would not have sent me away.' Her voice grew stronger with an echo of what might have been indignation. Lina took a small towel from her shoulder and laid it neatly across her knees. Then she lifted his foot and placed it on the towel, her movements sure and deft.

Sayid watched as she patted his foot dry then propped it, heel down on her thigh. With a firm, rhythmic movement she rubbed her thumbs over his sole, finding and working pressure points. Sayid felt warmth rise and spread, not only through his foot but his whole body. His tired eyes flickered and his aching muscles eased as pleasure rushed through him.

'You've done this before.'

'For my father.' Her features softened a fraction.

'Not your uncle?'

Instantly she stiffened, her mouth turning down at the corners and her forehead crinkling. 'No. It would not be appropriate. My aunt specifically forbade me to touch any of my male relatives.'

'There is more than your uncle?'

Her thumbs pressed so hard that the massage bordered on pain rather than pleasure. 'My uncle and aunt have three sons.'

'And you wanted to touch them?' For some reason Sayid disliked the idea.

'Ha! I'd rather touch a flea-ridden, spitting camel with diarrhoea than one of them.'

Sayid bit down a smile, weariness abating as curiosity rose. His demure little gift wasn't nearly as demure as she seemed.

'I see. *They* wanted to touch you.'

Lina nodded, her nostrils flaring in distaste. Her breasts rose high against his shirt as she breathed hard.

'They accused *me* of leading them on! Of tempting and teasing, when I never even *looked* at them. I avoided them as much as I could. But that wasn't enough. They said I wore perfume deliberately to entice them. That they could smell it when I left my room and it was an invitation for them to follow me.'

In her indignation Lina had forgotten to be cowed or careful. Fire flashed in her fine eyes and her cheeks blushed a soft rose.

Though he deplored their behaviour, Sayid understood too easily why her cousins found her such a temptation. Nervous and cowed she was lovely. Animated, she was glorious.

Even he, bound by his obligation as her ruler, as her host, and by his own honour, felt the dangerous undertow of attraction.

She was young, vulnerable and in his care. Unlike his dead uncle, Sayid didn't believe people should be given as gifts or treated as expendable.

No wonder her relatives had packed her off to the capital. To keep temptation away from the males of her family. He guessed there was little love lost between Lina and her aunt and uncle.

'Were there no other relatives willing to take you in?'

Her gaze dropped. She concentrated on drying his other foot and massaging it. Again Sayid felt the tug and release of taut muscles and tendons, and a glorious feeling of well-being. He'd never had a foot massage and was rapidly suspecting it might be addictive. Yet to his consternation the stirring in his loins indicated an inconvenient but growing arousal at odds with that wave of relaxation.

'My uncle moved his family into my father's house. And I have no other relatives. Even if there were, my mother…'

She paused so long Sayid wondered if she'd continue.

'My mother had been a dancer. Much younger than my father. She was not…approved of locally. No one else came forward to offer me a home when my father died.'

Sayid stared at her downcast face, at bone-deep beauty that even tightly pursed lips and a scowl couldn't mar.

With a nation to rule, a government to revamp and peace to establish, Sayid didn't have time for one lost girl.

Yet nor could he dismiss her. An orphan, without a family who'd care for her and, by the sound of it, a town that didn't want her, that was biased against her because of her mother, she'd been given away like a commodity. That easy disregard for people without the means to protect or support themselves was something he abhorred. He'd seen it too often under his uncle's rule.

He thrust aside the weary voice that protested responsibility for the nation was enough, without taking personal responsibility for a stray female too. A female who, given his powerful reaction, was surely trouble.

Yet she had no options, no home.

Who else would take responsibility if not her Emir?

Sayid took his obligations seriously.

'Thank you for the massage, Lina.' He withdrew from her touch, ignoring the tingle along his skin and the urge to let her minister to him with those supple hands.

Sayid sat straighter. He would *not* act on this burgeoning desire.

'Now.' He rose and she did too, again with that sinuous grace that drew the eye and made him think inevitably about a soft female body moving against his. His groin tightened. 'You can retire.' His voice was gruff. 'I'll see you tomorrow. My secretary will schedule a time.'

Her fine eyebrows arched in surprise. Then she smiled, a real smile, unlike that stilted curve of the lips she'd given him originally. The effect was instantaneous. Heat blasted him, feeding an urgent hunger he should be too worn out to experience.

Yet now he didn't feel worn out. He felt aroused.

'Thank you, sir. You won't regret this.' She actually bounced on the balls of her feet, as if from excitement.

Then she bowed herself out, a diminutive figure who should have looked comical with his shirt hanging loose over those filmy skirts. Instead his gaze locked on her in a mixture of fascination and pure, searing lust.

Seventeen. She's only seventeen.

Yet there was no mistaking that electric energy, the thunder in his blood and the heaviness in his groin.

Sayid raked his fingers across his scalp and swore.

Apart from her stunning looks, Lina wasn't like the women he chose for himself.

They were experienced and independent. Passionate enough to appreciate his demanding sex drive and sophisticated enough not to linger. He allowed himself no more than a week of intense carnal pleasure at a time before returning to his onerous responsibilities. It was part of his stringent private control system— giving free rein to his erotic appetites once in a while, then sublimating them while he focused on his work.

Mostly his lovers were foreigners wanting a taste of the exotic in the form of a hereditary prince. And most were blonde. His tastes didn't run to country-bred brunettes.

Until now.

Sayid swore again, exhaustion forgotten as he remembered those beguiling eyes and that curious mix of innocence and fire that made Lina far too alluring to a man who should know better.

He had to come up with a plan for her. A place for her to live.

Lina couldn't stay in the palace indefinitely.

His self-restraint only went so far.

CHAPTER THREE

LINA SHIFTED IN her seat. It was a very comfortable seat, but she'd been sitting in it for ages. The Emir's serious-eyed secretary had looked down his nose at her and warned she'd have a long wait, since the Emir had many important appointments. Far more important, he implied, with a comprehensive glance, than dealing with some tawdry dancing girl.

Lina wanted to tell him the clothes she wore weren't her choice. She hadn't been permitted to bring her own clothes with her to the palace, only the outfits her aunt had provided.

She'd stared straight back at the secretary, refusing to drop her gaze, and let him huff and puff. Eventually he'd led her into the library, motioned to a chair and left.

Now, finally, Lina could stand the temptation no more. She'd never seen so many books. They lined three walls. Surely that was more than any person could ever read in a lifetime.

Quietly, she got up and tiptoed to the nearest shelf. The covers were beautiful, leather and fabric in all the hues of a rainbow. Some tall and slim. Others short and stumpy. She reached out and trailed her fingers over one, then another, then another.

Imagine all the secrets hidden in these books. All the nuggets of knowledge. All the explanations of scientific marvels and history. And stories, so many stories contained in this massive collection. Wonderful stories such as her mother had told her and many more besides. The idea left her giddy with the possibilities.

With a quick look over her shoulder, Lina selected a book. Its cover was hard and green with gilt lettering. The secretary hadn't said she couldn't touch.

Carefully she slid it out, testing its weight on her hands. She opened it to find gorgeously coloured pictures of plants. A few she recognised, ones that grew in the foothills near her home. Others were unfamiliar. Her fingers traced the delicate shape of one beautiful flower. Its petals were a dark red that looked so real it might have been plucked fresh this morning.

Finally, when she'd looked her fill, she put the book back and moved along the shelf, selecting another at random. This one had a cover of red. Inside there were no pictures, but—

'Lina.'

She spun, almost dropping the precious book as she started.

The Emir closed the door behind him. Last night, in the warm glow of his lamplit bedroom, he'd thrown her off balance. She'd told herself it was shock because she'd seen so much of his handsome, sculpted body. More than any woman expected to see of a man who was not her husband.

Yet that same thrill of excitement ran through her veins as he crossed the room towards her with that easy stride. The same breathlessness at his sheer masculine beauty and that aura of power he wore as surely as the fine white robes. His face, against the pale fabric, was bronze and arrestingly handsome. His eyes dark and penetrating.

And she knew exactly what he was like beneath his clothing. The moulded muscles, the hard, intriguing line of his shoulders. The wisp of black hair that bisected his flat belly and dipped below his trousers.

That explained why her heart hammered too fast and why, low in her body, she felt a rush of unfamiliar molten heat. It was reaction to him as a man, not as her ruler.

The realisation brought a flush to her cheeks and she hurriedly looked down at the book, open in her hands.

'It's good to see someone making use of the library. I doubt my uncle ever opened the books and I haven't had time yet. Is it something interesting?' His tone was gentle. Clearly he tried to put her at ease. As if she were his equal, not his…possession. Her breath hitched on the thought.

He stopped before her and every hair on her body prickled in awareness.

'I…don't know. I just opened it.'

There was a long pause. Then he reached out and lifted the book from her hands. But instead of keeping it, he merely turned it up the other way and gave it back to her.

Lina stared down at the lines of writing, warmth rising in her cheeks. She swallowed but didn't look up.

'Lina?'

'Yes, sir?'

'Can you read?' She heard the whisper of kindness in his voice, a note that reminded her, abruptly, of her long-dead mother. For even her father, though not mean or cruel, had never been tender.

A lump formed in her throat.

'Lina?' That tone, though gentle, compelled. She felt the force of his will drag her head up till her gaze collided with his. She shivered as fire and ice made her skin tingle and her backbone stiffen.

'No, sir.' Shame swamped her. She hated to admit the deficiency. It seemed to reinforce every cliché that had been thrown at her and her mother by her father's relatives and many of their neighbours. As if their lack of learning was a character flaw rather than a lack of opportunity.

'But there are schools in your town. I've seen them.' The Emir's brow knotted.

Lina nodded. She'd pleaded to be allowed to attend. But it had not been deemed appropriate.

'My father didn't believe it necessary for females to attend school. My mother wanted me to go, but she died when I was young and there was no one else to persuade my father.' She paused, feeling it necessary to explain. Her father hadn't been evil, just set in his ways. And he'd been disappointed that his only child was a girl. 'He had very traditional views.'

Lina's mother had been his second wife, twenty years his junior. She'd been beautiful, clever and charming, but faced prejudice because poverty and lack of education had forced her into becoming a dancer, performing in public before her marriage. That prejudice tainted Lina too, as if despite her careful upbringing, her morals were questionable because of her mother's previous profession.

'Do you want to learn?'

Lina blinked up at the grave face before her. Was he serious?

If it were her uncle or one of his sons asking, she'd expect some sort of teasing trick, to raise her hopes then dash them. But this was the Emir. The man who'd listened to her last night when he could have ignored her. Who'd been polite and almost gentle, despite his obvious fatigue.

The man who'd allowed her to go to her own bed, alone and untouched, instead of doing any of the things she'd been told he'd demand of her.

She hadn't slept all night, going over and over each word, each gesture and nuance in her mind. The more she'd remembered, the more the glow of warmth inside her built.

'Of course! I tried to find someone to teach me. But it didn't work out.'

She'd made the mistake of asking one of her cousins. The quiet, scholarly one who didn't make brash jokes in her presence and who'd seemed almost pleasant. Except their 'lesson' had lasted about five minutes before his hands started to wander. Then he'd grabbed her and tried to kiss her and Lina had never been so glad to see her aunt as when she'd burst in, even though it meant Lina was locked in her room for the next week as punishment.

Her hands shook so much she closed the book and put it down on the shelf beside her. 'Would you...? Could I *really* learn to read and write?'

Hope nosedived at his suddenly fierce expression. As if her excitement displeased him. For a long moment he stared at her, his mouth a grim line. Then he nodded curtly and swung away to take a seat behind his imposing desk.

'Of course it's possible. In fact, it's necessary if you're going to make your way in the world.'

He gestured for her to take the seat before him. It made her feel a little like she had as a child, called before her father to account for some misdeed. Except, despite the shimmer of tension in the air and the hint of anger in the Emir's tensed jaw, there was compassion in his eyes.

'Clearly you can't stay here in the palace.'

'But I—'

A raised palm stopped her words and she shivered, realising she'd been about to argue with the man who held not only her fate, but her nation's, in his palm. Her aunt had been right. Lina needed to curb her tongue.

'I don't keep a harem and when I want a woman it will never be someone forced to attend me.'

A shiver rolled through her, pulling her flesh tight. In that instant she was sucked straight back to those long nights of terror, waiting to be called before the Emir, to do whatever he commanded.

Yet now Lina felt that, if this man smiled and spoke to her in the smoky, caressing tone he'd used a few minutes earlier, she'd go to him willingly. She might be nervous about learning first-hand about sex, but her shimmy of excitement hinted she'd be avid to learn if Sayid Badawi taught her.

The realisation stopped her tongue.

'However,' he said, his voice serious, 'you're now my responsibility. I can't send you back to your family, since they treated you so badly.' His eyes flashed and, despite his even tone, she realised he was very, very angry. With her aunt and uncle? The grim line of his jaw accentuated the heavy beat of a pulse in his throat and she was struck with the idea they would suffer for bundling her off here.

Lina felt her eyes grow round and her mouth sag open. She knew because she'd overheard them speaking, that her aunt and uncle believed sending her to the palace would not only remove her from their sons but gain them favour with the Emir.

The old Emir. Not the new one. Sayid Badawi was not cut from the same cloth as his uncle.

'Given the circumstances in which you arrived, you can't stay in the palace. People would misconstrue your...role.'

Lina wasn't exactly sure what misconstrue meant. She assumed the Emir didn't want people believing she was his concubine.

After all, she was nothing but an uneducated provincial. Even a woman as inexperienced as Lina understood that this man, with his power, wealth and chiselled looks would have his pick of stunning women. He'd only have to click his fingers and they'd flock to him like doves to grain.

Why, he probably already had a lover, perhaps secreted here in the palace.

Heat flushed Lina's cheeks as she remembered where her mind had wandered last night as she'd thought about the Emir, his kindness and his charisma. His cedar wood and bitter orange scent that made her feel curiously giddy. That zing of awareness when she touched him.

Of course he had a woman. It was ridiculous to

think he'd ever want someone like her. Someone who didn't even know how to hold a book the right way up!

'I've decided to treat you as my ward.'

'Your ward?' She looked up and found herself snared by dark-as-night eyes. Another tiny shiver scudded down her spine.

'I will be responsible for you until you can make your own way in the world.'

Slowly Lina nodded, biting down a question about how she was meant to do that when she only had domestic training.

'Like an uncle,' he added, as if to clarify.

Lina blinked. Anyone less like an uncle she couldn't imagine. He was far too young for a start. Closer to her age than her uncle's. Besides, she couldn't imagine what she felt for the Emir was at all appropriate between niece and uncle.

'You understand?'

Did he think her dim-witted because she couldn't read the words in his precious books?

'Yes.' She clasped her hands before her. 'You will act as my guardian.'

'Precisely.' He nodded, then sat back in his chair as if pleased that point was understood. 'Now what would you like to do?'

'Sir?'

'What would you like for the future?'

Lina tried not to gape and probably failed.

No one ever, in her whole life, had asked what she wanted her future to be. It had always been assumed that her father would find her a suitable husband and she'd devote herself to looking after him and the family they'd have. Or, if her aunt were to be believed, she'd become a dancing girl or worse, pandering to the desires of men.

The enormity of the question stole her voice.

Eventually he spoke again. 'You must have some desire. Some dream.'

Suddenly Lina remembered those childish hopes she'd once harboured. Hopes encouraged by the foreign archaeologists who'd worked for years near her home. They'd been entertained in her house when she was young, and, to her delight, there had even been women archaeologists. Lina had spent years tagging along behind them, before she was considered too old for such freedoms.

'Lina? What is it you want?' That deep voice yanked her back to the present.

The foolishness of those old hopes hit her anew. She could never do what she'd dreamed. And yet, here she was, sitting with the man who ruled Halarq, a man who'd brought peace to her nation, and he was asking her what she desired. *Asking.* Surely anything was possible here with this extraordinary man?

'I want to learn,' she said before she lost her nerve. 'To read and go to classes and find out about the world.' Her throat constricted at the daring of what she asked but she hurried on. 'And I want to visit France and America.'

There. It was out. Her breath came in rough little pants and her fingers trembled against the carved wooden arms of the chair. She knew she'd been too daring. But she'd been unable to resist.

'Why those countries?' Instead of berating her for not requesting something sensible, like an apprenticeship to a seamstress, the Emir leaned forward as if curious. 'It would be hard when you don't speak the language.'

'But I do!' She beamed at him. 'At least I used to. I spent time with the foreigners digging up the past in the old city ruins beyond my town. I have a good memory and they said I'm quick with languages.'

Clearly he wasn't convinced. Yet nor did he dismiss her claim. Instead he sat in brooding silence, his elbows on the desk and fingers steepled beneath his chin.

Lina barely dared to breathe for fear of disturbing him as time stretched from seconds into long minutes.

'Very well.' Finally he sat back. A smile skated across his face and Lina caught her breath. In repose his face was serious yet handsome. But when he smiled it felt like angels danced in her soul.

'I won't promise America or France, but I can give you the opportunity to learn.' He paused as if considering. 'My secretary will arrange a teacher. If, by the end of a week, that teacher confirms you're working hard and willing to learn, you will have the opportunity to go to school.'

Excitement was the buzz of a thousand bees in her bloodstream. 'Sir, I can't thank you enough. I—'

His raised hand cut her off. His expression turned serious. 'It's inevitable that gossip will get out about how you came here and about our...*relationship*.'

He said the word as if he tasted something unpleasant and instantly Lina's warm glow subsided. 'Given that, *if* you show promise, you will attend school outside Halarq.'

Lina nodded, torn between delight and the need

to pinch herself to check she was awake. 'But won't it be expensive?'

Instantly his gaze, which had fixed on a spot in the middle distance, zeroed in on her. Once more Lina felt that keen scrutiny, as if he looked at her but saw more than anyone else ever had.

'Fortunately I can afford it.' A ghost of a smile hovered around his firm mouth. '*If* you work hard, I will sponsor your education.'

'But how will I repay you?' The words erupted before she could hold them back.

The Emir's eyebrows rose. In surprise because she continued to speak without being invited? Yet he didn't seem angry. Was that approval in his gleaming eyes?

'You cannot simply accept this gift?'

Lina bit her lip, considering carefully. His Royal Highness the Emir of Halarq was a powerful man, accustomed to having his every word obeyed. Yet her conscience—or was it the pride her aunt complained of?—told her she had to set limits to this kindness.

'I would be honoured, sir. Yet that same honour compels me to acknowledge my great obligation to you. It's an obligation I must repay. We aren't kin. I have no call on your charity.'

Lina's heart thudded in her chest, her pulse rushing so fast through her body she felt light-headed.

For what seemed an age those piercing eyes, darker now and unreadable as polished obsidian, bored into her. Then, abruptly, he nodded.

'So be it. If this turns out as I hope, you'll be a shining example of change in Halarq. I intend to modernise our country through education, among other things. Work hard, learn, and on your return you can repay my generosity by helping to promote the value of education in those areas where people still refuse to send their daughters to school.'

He glanced at his watch and shoved his chair back from the desk.

Instantly Lina scrambled to her feet before sinking into a low bow, her heart swelling fit to burst. 'I promise to study hard, sir.' She'd make him proud, no matter what it took.

'Excellent.' With that he turned and strode from the room.

Four and a half years later Lina stepped off the plane a different woman.

Which was apt since the country she returned to had changed too.

The airport had expanded for a start, with a new streamlined terminal building and space for many more planes. The road into the city was a revelation— wide, straight and well-surfaced. It was even lined with rows of date palms and other trees.

A new hospital sat in spacious landscaped grounds at a major road junction and a university was under construction nearby. Across the city cranes testified to a programme of renewal.

The driver who'd met her kept up a flow of informative chatter in response to her queries. That marked a change too, for when she'd left Halarq she couldn't imagine a male driver speaking more than was absolutely necessary to a woman. Though, to be fair, her experience was limited. She'd grown up in a rural province before her uncle had brought her to the capital. She'd rarely been in a car before she'd left her homeland. And this wasn't an ordinary car but a limousine with the Emir's crest on the door.

Lina felt a rogue shiver of heat through her insides at the thought that he'd sent one of his drivers to collect her.

Had he personally arranged it? Or had one of his staff done it without being asked?

Did the Emir even remember her?

In all those years years he'd sent not a word, though she knew the school staff had sent regular reports to the palace. For the first year, homesick and overwhelmed by the changes in her life, she'd have given anything for a word from him. In her loneliness the Emir had grown in her imagination, filling the empty places in her soul. He was protector, hero, saviour... and something else she couldn't put a name to.

In the years she'd been away, bombarded with new experiences and places, new people and ideas, he'd remained a constant. A lodestar, the single reference point connecting her to Halarq and the world she'd left behind.

Which, she realised with a grimace, was dangerous. She was nothing to him. Once she'd fulfilled her end of their bargain she'd never see him again.

Pining over the Emir and wondering whether he approved of her choices and achievements wasn't sensible.

He'd probably forgotten her. No doubt his officious secretary kept a watching brief on the little social experiment that was Lina. For though His Royal Highness had been kind, she understood he'd only looked for a solution that would remove her from the palace and feed into his plans to modernise Halarq. He simply hadn't wanted her.

Nothing new there. To her father she'd been a disappointment because of her gender. To her aunt and uncle an inconvenience. To the Emir a problem to be solved.

Tangled emotions knotted Lina's stomach. Anxiety definitely. Though she'd survived and eventually thrived in her Swiss school, she knew what it was to be utterly alone. She longed for connection. To belong, to a place and to people, or at least one person.

Savagely Lina cut off that thought.

She'd daydreamed of the Emir, so tall and handsome, for too long. She was no teenager now. There'd be no swooning over him, or for that matter, any man.

Once her obligation to the Emir was fulfilled, she had a career to build. An income to earn. A life to enjoy.

The limousine turned off the teeming street and onto the private road that led up from the old town to the citadel. Above, its coral-coloured walls rising from the sheer rock, rose the Emir's palace. A silver and blue banner over the gate whipped in the breeze, proclaiming the Emir was in residence.

Lina clasped her hands tight in her lap, trying to still the rising tide of excitement and trepidation that quickened her pulse.

She'd thank him for the wonderful thing he'd done in giving her an education. She'd throw herself into whatever PR tasks he devised to promote education and, as soon as she could, remove herself from his orbit.

She smiled. That was settled.

Except, as so often in life, it didn't work out that way.

* * *

Sayid exchanged farewells with the fiercely bearded provincial leader then watched him and his entourage bow themselves out through the wide doors of beaten copper.

Rolling his head back, he tried to relieve the stiffness of too many hours sitting in the formal audience chamber. It had been a long afternoon.

He disliked this echoing room with its lavish decorations and raised dais that set him apart from everyone. But he'd made so many reforms in such a short time, he listened when his aides advised he should retain the traditional space for meetings with provincial sheikhs. He worked hard to steer them into change on significant issues. Where he worked was not, to his mind, important. If retaining a show of the old customs made them more comfortable, so be it.

He was getting to his feet when the chamberlain appeared in the doorway. He wasn't alone.

Sayid sank back on the jewelled throne, his hands curling over the gilded lion heads on the arms.

Suddenly alert, his eagerness to go dissipated as he took in the figure walking beside the chamberlain. Slim, curvaceous, delectably feminine, though her fitted skirt and jacket in jade green covered her from neck to knee.

Late afternoon sun lit her from behind, which had the twofold effect of making it difficult to read her features while highlighting her lush curves in loving detail.

High heels tapped demurely across the inlaid floor and Sayid had time to note her glossy dark hair was pulled severely back and up.

She halted in the middle of the room. Her eyes were downcast, as was traditional in Halarq on meeting the Emir. Yet it was rare for westerners to know that. She was well-prepared.

He sat forward, intrigued that a lone western woman should seek an audience.

'You may approach.'

The pair walked slowly towards him and Sayid found himself watching with appreciation the gentle undulation of her hips as she paced in those high heels. She wore no jewellery but that only accentuated the purity of her sculpted beauty. High cheekbones, eyes set on an intriguing slant, full lips, slender throat.

Heat crawled up from Sayid's belly to clog his chest. A blast of fire shot straight to his loins. His hands tightened on the carved chair as she stopped before him, still with downcast eyes. She was one of the most beautiful, elegant women he'd ever seen. And Sayid had known many.

Yet something about her feathered his nape with a cold brush of warning.

Here, he sensed, lay trouble.

The chamberlain spoke. 'Sire, I am pleased to bring before you…'

The woman's jaw tipped high, her gaze rising to meet his and the chamberlain's words were lost in the heavy thrum of Sayid's pulse as he looked down into eyes as velvety as a drift of mountain violets. Holding his gaze, she dipped into a curtsey that was the epitome of grace.

Shock hammered. His blood rushed, drowning all noise.

Lina. Little Lina.

Sayid remembered her as pretty. Had told himself imagination had embroidered her charms. It had been the forbidden piquancy of finding himself her *master*, free to do as he wished with her, that had turned a passably attractive teenager into something special in his mind.

He'd been wrong. She *was* something special. More, she was extraordinary.

Not just because of her beauty. The way that clear-eyed stare met his, the hint of boldness behind the mask of politeness, communicated directly with him on a personal level. A level that made his belly tense and his calm crack.

'Welcome back to Halarq.' He kept his voice as grave as his expression. She might have knocked him sideways for an instant but Sayid would never let that show.

'Thank you, sir.' She bowed low in a move as formal and graceful as that of any courtier.

He refused to let his eyes track her trim frame, but it was too late. Her image was imprinted on his brain. 'You've grown up.'

Her gaze met his, setting off a buzz of response at the base of his spine. Then her lips twitched into a far too appealing half-smile and she shrugged. 'It happens to all of us.' She paused, as if waiting for him to respond. 'I just turned twenty-two last week.'

Better, far better than seventeen.

The sly voice in his mind was full of insinuation. Of anticipation. But he'd set himself up as her protector, her guardian. *Because she had no one else.*

Sayid knew what could happen to women who had

no one to champion them. Especially beautiful, desirable women.

It was why he'd sent Lina away. Not only to pursue her education, but to keep her out of reach. He might be changing his country, one step at a time, to ensure *all* his people had the rights of free citizens, but he was still a man.

A man with a formidable appetite for pleasure.

Knowing that was a family trait, seeing its devastating effect on his uncle, who'd never learned to resist temptation, Sayid had striven to contain that side of his nature.

Yet he looked at Lina and something raw and ravenous stirred in his belly. Something uncivilised and unrepentantly greedy that spoke of want and the need to possess. It was a burn in his gut. A sharpness on his tongue. A tightening of his body.

Just like that! As if the rules he'd set for himself no longer existed. As if she wasn't in his care.

Damn!

Years before he'd done what he could to protect her. According to Halarqi custom, since she'd been given into his keeping, Lina *belonged* to him. From that moment he was the head of her family. In his people's eyes, and the law's, he was her lord. Her master. Potentially her lover.

To his shame, the idea still sent an illicit thrill through him.

Yet, to his credit he'd done what a decent, civilised man would do—embracing his responsibility and becoming her guardian, sending her away.

He'd forgotten she was due to return today. Plus he'd assumed the years would be enough to sever this startling, impossible tug of desire. That he'd have become immune or she'd have grown ordinary.

Neither had happened.

Surely it was a malicious, mocking Fate that had allowed him to send away a child, only to receive in return a woman so flagrantly desirable.

Sayid forced a smile. 'Congratulations on reaching such an advanced age.' He stood, turning to the chamberlain. 'That will be all for now. My ward and I have matters to discuss.'

CHAPTER FOUR

IF LINA HAD expected a warm welcome from her self-styled guardian, she'd have been disappointed.

The tight curve of his mouth could be classed as a smile, but it didn't reach his eyes. Those gleamed as cool and impenetrable as black onyx. Yet something about the quality of that look sent a tremor of yearning through her insides.

Severely she told herself she hadn't expected warmth.

It was just that he'd been kind.

He'd treated her, not as an encumbrance or an embarrassment, but as a person who mattered.

When she looked at him she felt something like the prickle of delight she'd known years before in her home on the edge of the desert. She'd looked at the night sky and lost herself in the beauty of the diamond-bright wash of stars. Then she'd felt small and vulnerable but at the same time exultant, as if the vast night sky had touched her with a tiny spark of its magic.

Lina was too old for girlish fantasies about a handsome sheikh. Even though he'd swept in and rescued her. Even though such fantasies had been her solace and her rock as she grappled with life beyond Halarq and everything she knew.

Yet, to her dismay, she discovered fantasies weren't so easy to banish. She looked into those midnight eyes, heard the warm burr of his voice, and felt it again, that swirl of starlight and wonder. That ripple of hyper-consciousness. Even the contrast of his spare, burnished flesh against pristine white robes caught and held her gaze. And the honed, arrogant but beautiful angles and planes of his face.

He'd altered in four and a half years. His shoulders seemed even wider than before, his chest deeper. There were new lines around his eyes and mouth too, but they only accentuated the masculine charisma of that strong face.

For one mad instant, when she saw a pulse pound at his temple and those broad shoulders stiffen, she'd thought he, too, was affected. But that was her imagination running riot. A second look confirmed she was wrong.

He led her to a pair of opulent antique chairs positioned on the far side of the room. They were a formal few metres apart, slightly turned to make the best of the view from the citadel, down over the ancient sprawling city.

'Is it good to be home?'

Lina turned in her seat to find him watching her closely. A shiver skated through her at the intensity of his regard. She sat straighter.

'I…it feels strange.' Though what felt most strange was hearing him speak of *home*. As if she truly belonged though she was an outsider here. 'I don't really know the city. I was only here a short time.'

His sleek black eyebrows lifted. 'You would rather return to your old town? Your old home?'

'No. No!' The shiver that tracked her spine this time had nothing to do with the man sitting across from her. Her fingers curled tight in her lap as she leaned closer. 'Please don't send me back. There's no place for me there.'

She paused, pushing down the rising fear that she'd be made to return to the family who despised her. For years she hadn't entertained the possibility. Surely the Emir had saved her from that?

'I'm sure I'll adjust quickly to life in the capital.'

She'd adapted to moving from a provincial town to an international school in Switzerland. To make matters worse, it wasn't just any school, but one patronised by the wealthy and privileged. It taught not only the usual academic subjects, but all the other things deemed necessary for a young woman about to take her privileged place in society. Presumably some officious secretary, on receiving the orders to enrol her in a school at royal expense, had automatically searched for the best, because only the best was ever provided for the Emir.

The other girls, all from wealthy families, had initially treated her as a freak. A freak who barely spoke their languages. Who couldn't even read or write.

She'd been a figure of fun, the butt of malicious jokes and cruelty. It had only been in her last two years, as the oldest pupil there, that she'd found her place and become a mentor for the younger girls. She'd worked hard and shown true flair in her passion for languages and history, even if her writing was still laborious.

'You're certain you don't want to return?' She looked up to see his eyes narrowed on her, his hard, handsome face close to a frown. 'There hasn't been a softening in your relationship with your aunt and uncle?'

Lina snorted at the absurdity of the idea, then ducked her head, apologising. People did *not* snort in front of national leaders.

'I take it that's a no.'

She looked up in time to catch a glimmer in his eyes that she couldn't identify. It made him seem more approachable. More like the man she'd met years ago who'd been stern yet gentle. Instantly Lina sank back in her chair, relief buzzing in her veins.

'I've had no contact with them since the day my uncle left me at the servants' entrance to the palace.' For all they knew she could have spent the intervening years warming the Emir's bed as his concubine.

Heat swept Lina's breasts and throat and she moistened her lips as her throat dried.

Not in embarrassment at the idea, but because the thought of sharing Sayid Badawi's bed appealed too much.

She'd once glimpsed behind the serious visage and imposing title to the virile, fascinating, kind man beyond. And she couldn't seem to cure herself of the yearning to know more of him. *Experience* more.

As if he'd be interested in someone like her!

His stare didn't waver, nor did he feel the need to fill the silence. She wondered frantically what he read in her face.

Lina had devoured every story she could find about him. They painted a portrait of a strong, determined leader, a man with a vision for his country. And a man who, discreetly but definitely, had an eye for beautiful women.

Could he see how she felt about him? Did he sense that tickle of heated awareness? She'd never felt it with any other man. Only him.

As she watched, his hands gripped the arms of his chair. His ring of authority, a wide band of gold inset with a glowing cabochon ruby, caught the light.

Lina's pulse throbbed but curiously, as she met that midnight gaze, her heartbeat seemed to slow, grow ponderous and heavy. The air thickened, making her lungs chug hard to draw in oxygen.

Though they didn't sit close, Lina could swear she inhaled that spicy, sensual aroma she'd smelled only once before. Citrus and cedar wood with a darker note of something she registered as warm male skin.

Her skin tingled, as if from a phantom caress, and she swayed forward, drawn by the expression in his eyes.

Abruptly he moved. His gaze jerked from hers towards the door. Instantly Lina felt the current of energy holding her grow taut, snap and disintegrate as surely as if he'd flicked off a switch.

'Very well. You'll stay here at the palace for now. Later we'll talk about your future and make some decisions.'

Still reeling from the impact of his stare, Lina was slow to speak. She should have said she'd already decided what she wanted to do with her future. She wanted to train as an interpreter. But he glanced at his watch and she kept her mouth shut. There'd be time enough later.

'I'm informed you were a conscientious pupil.' Was that a twitch at one corner of his mouth? A half smile? 'I congratulate you, Lina. You did well when many would have found the transition too hard.'

'It was hard.' In the beginning it had been awful. Only the kindness of her teachers, and the knowledge that this was her one chance to pursue her dream, had kept her there. 'But it was worth it. I can't thank you enough.' She moved forward in her seat. 'Truly, it was a wonderful thing you did for me. I—'

'Excellent. I'm pleased you found it valuable and that you made the most of it.' He dismissed her thanks as if his generosity didn't matter. But he'd opened a whole new world to her. She'd never forget that.

The Emir rose and so did Lina, stifling disappointment that their interview was so cursory.

'See my secretary and he'll brief you. You'll begin by meeting staff from the Department of Education. I want you involved in their work with local communities. But we'll see how it goes.'

'That sounds wonderful. I'm looking forward to it.' Lina smiled wide and saw him blink. Was he surprised at her enthusiasm? 'I'm ready to help and I'm enthusiastic about the benefits of education. I'm sure it will work out well. I enjoy meeting people and talking with them.'

Under her uncle's roof that had got her into trouble, but recently Lina had been delighted to discover others valued her ability to connect with people. At school they'd called her a people person, as if it were a positive thing instead of a flaw.

'Good.' The Emir inclined his head. 'I look forward to hearing about your progress.'

* * *

But Lina learned he didn't want personal updates. In the ten days that followed, as she found her way more confidently around the palace, and began to attend some of the school and community visits, she rarely saw the Emir.

Occasionally she'd see him stride down the corridor with that distinctive loose-hipped, shoulders back walk, full of confidence and athletic grace. Every time her heart would skip and her mouth would dry.

Occasionally he'd spot her and nod or raise a hand in greeting. But every time he'd be on his way somewhere, accompanied by his secretary or some official.

On the positive side, she slowly found her feet in this new world. She realised quickly that her role promoting education was a manufactured position. There were professionals who already did that. Clearly the Emir had created this job to give her something useful to do.

She hated being treated as a charity case, even if that was what she was. But she was grateful for the chance to salve her pride by contributing even a little to his schemes for the country. Gradually she began to feel as if she *was* helping.

When the Emir's secretary, Makram, told her she was invited to attend a dinner in the grand dining hall, she thought at first it was a mistake. But Makram didn't make mistakes. And unlike his predecessor, he didn't look down on her, so this wasn't a joke at her expense. Instead he advised on the dress code and referred to an allowance the Emir had set up for her at a local bank.

Lina's chin lifted at that news. She'd accepted enough of the Emir's generosity. She'd saved most of the spending money she'd been sent while overseas. She couldn't accept more. Already she was housed in unimaginable luxury.

Now Lina stroked her hands down the silky dress she'd never before worn, watching the way it hugged her figure in the mirror. She swallowed hard. Did it cling too much? It hadn't seemed to when she'd made it in Switzerland. She twirled, the knee-length skirt flaring a little, making her wish she could go dancing. No, the dress was feminine but not revealing. The scooped neck merely hinted at her cleavage, and she'd even covered her bare arms with a pretty shawl she'd found in the markets.

Excitement vied with trepidation and Lina grinned at the woman in the mirror. She was going to a royal dinner party, as a guest, not a servant!

Would he notice her?

Would he speak to her?

Her heart danced a jig of anticipation.

She spun on her heel and swept through the door, ignoring the inner voice that warned her to be careful.

She'd been careful and conscientious for years. Tonight she intended to enjoy herself.

'I'm pleased you're enjoying your stay.' Sayid smiled at the foreign professor, one of a team visiting to advise on setting up state-of-the-art research laboratories at the new university. 'When your meetings are over you must visit the desert. I'll have my staff arrange it.'

The man nodded and began to talk enthusiastically about the new plant recently identified in Halarq's barren heartland. Of how a substance extracted from it might provide a breakthrough for medical research.

Sayid nodded, drawing another guest into the conversation. It would be fascinating if he hadn't already been briefed on the details.

And if his attention wasn't constantly diverted by the sound of laughter from the other side of the royal reception room where guests mingled before dinner.

He was pleased the guests enjoyed themselves, especially as they were such a disparate group. But it wasn't pleasure he felt whenever the sound of good cheer reached him. It was something unsettling.

For amidst the deeper notes of male amusement came the sound of Lina's voice, pure and true as a songbird's, a silvery trill of delight that undid something inside him.

He hadn't heard her laugh before. Had rarely seen her smile. Tonight, experiencing both, he found himself constantly distracted. Not because she was overloud. But because he wanted to be there, beside her, basking in the joy that bubbled from her.

Another laugh, this time in response to a murmured male comment and Sayid felt jealousy slice his belly.

Jealousy! Of his own secretary, Makram? And, he darted a quick glance across the room, a junior member of the American Embassy staff, and a foreign businessman.

'They're having a good time.' Sayid turned to see his friend, the Minister for Education, nodding towards the laughter. 'Your Lina is a breath of fresh air.'

His Lina?

For a second Sayid's brain stuck on the pronoun. *His.* 'You know my ward?'

'We met yesterday at a community centre near the main souk. Where the new school is being built.'

Sayid nodded. The area was in the heart of the oldest part of the city, its population a mix of highly paid professionals and urban poor. 'I know it.'

'I thought it clever of you to send her along with my staff. The local women related to her more than to officials. Perhaps it was the way she rolled up her sleeves and joined them in baking bread at the communal oven.'

Sayid's gaze slewed across the room. Lina had her head back, laughing. When was the last time he'd heard uninhibited laughter at one of these events?

Her throat looked slender and sublimely elegant. The shawl of rich blue and gold had slipped down her bare arms. His gaze traced the outline of her breasts in a dress that gleamed richly, the colour of lapis lazuli. It reminded him of the gems in the royal treasury.

Lina looked as if she was born to wear silks and velvet, rubies and pearls.

She looked as if she belonged here.

He'd wondered if she'd hold her own tonight, but he needn't have worried. She seemed completely at ease. How far she'd come from the anxious, half-defiant teenager he'd first met.

'I didn't know she could cook.' But that wasn't true. She'd offered, hadn't she, to work in the kitchens or the laundry, rather than return to her uncle's house?

'I suspect she's a woman of many talents.'

Sayid's gaze narrowed, but he saw no salacious expression. If anything his friend looked paternally approving.

Slowly Sayid nodded. He could only agree. He'd been impressed by the reports he'd received from her school. Lina was hard-working and determined. She also had a reputation for honesty, sociability and kind-ness, especially valued by the staff and the younger homesick girls. There'd even been a suggestion of a position for her at the academy, should she ever want it.

'She has a way with people that's more effective than anything we've tried before.'

'Really?' Pride rose. He'd thought from the first Lina was far from ordinary. That she had potential it would be criminal not to encourage.

'You didn't realise?'

'I barely know her,' Sayid admitted, just as if he hadn't received regular reports over the years. 'She's spent a lot of time away.' At his friend's stare he added, 'But I agree, she can be quite…winning.'

'Definitely winning. She's charming. In the be-ginning I thought she'd be just a decorative addition to our team. But she proved me wrong. She listened to everyone's concerns and when she spoke it wasn't about what they ought or must do. It was about how school would help them and their children right now, not just in the distant future.' He nodded. 'We might all talk the same language but she speaks it in a way they can relate to.'

'She has a passion for education,' Sayid murmured. Plus she'd grown up, if not in poverty, since her fa-ther was Headman of his town, but without luxuries. He remembered her shining eyes when he'd agreed to provide an education. The ripple of delight he'd felt at her excitement.

'Not just education.' His friend nodded towards the animated group in conversation across the room. 'For life. And possibly for tall blond Americans.'

Sayid followed his glance. A handsome diplomat was leaning towards Lina and she gazed up as if enraptured.

An unseen fist rammed into Sayid's gut. Why had he allowed the American's name to be included on the guest list? He ignored the fact that it was his policy to invite foreign nationals to such evenings. Establishing better ties with the world beyond his country's borders was a priority.

Sayid turned back to his friend. 'If you'll excuse me. It's time I mingled with my other guests.'

Nodding acknowledgement on the way, pausing to chat here and there, it took Sayid an age to reach the group clustered nearest the door to the dining hall.

As he approached he heard a woman speaking English in an accent that summoned memories of drumming hoof beats and vast wide open spaces, not unlike Halarq.

Sayid frowned. He saw no other woman in the group, much less one with that distinctive Texan drawl. Only Lina, in a shimmering blue dress that gleamed subtly under the brilliant chandeliers. The spill of gilded light showcased each delectable curve and dip of that hourglass figure.

He swallowed, his throat suddenly parched. He preferred tall, leggy blondes, he reminded himself.

But his body wasn't listening.

'I'm afraid I'm not very good. My American friend would be rolling on the floor with laughter if she heard me now.' The accent disintegrated on the words, replaced by Lina's musical tones.

Sayid halted not far from Lina, stunned.

Lina was a mimic?

What other secrets did she hide?

Hungrily his gaze ate her up. Her hair was in a re-fined knot, her posture perfect, her manner easy and her clothes elegant and expensive-looking.

She was definitely no schoolgirl any more. The question that clawed at Sayid's gut now was what sort of woman she'd become.

Had the allowance he'd provided paid for the dress that had obviously been designed specifically for her? Or had some man—?

'No, no! You're great. What about me? Can you do my accent?' It was the American, leaning in, a lock of golden hair flopping over his boyishly handsome face.

Lina shook her head. 'I'm sorry. I have to hear an accent for longer before I can attempt it.' Yet even as she spoke, Sayid was fascinated to hear her vowels become clipped, her intonation change in an approxi-mation of the foreigner's.

So much for his concerns Lina might feel ner-vous. This was by far the most animated group in the room. Because of Lina. Even from here he sensed the charm that so dazzled her audience. She wasn't brash or pushy, just…vibrant.

'That's easily fixed.' The American's smile wid-ened. 'We can spend more time together. I'll share everything you want to know about Boston and…'

His words died as Sayid stepped into the group.

Beside him Lina stiffened and he heard the soft hitch of her breath. He told himself he'd simply sur-prised her, yet an unrepentant part of him hoped it was more, something akin to the instant charge of energy that zapped him whenever she was near. It sizzled now from his fingers, a mere hand span from hers, up his arm and through his body in a fiery shower of sparks.

'Your Highness.' The men bowed and Lina sank into a graceful curtsey as perfect as any ballerina's.

'I'm glad you're all enjoying the evening. I heard the laughter and was curious.'

'Ms Rahman was demonstrating her talent for accents.' It was the American who spoke, his eyes bright with unconcealed approval. 'She's very talented.'

'It's nothing, really.' Lina sounded breathless. 'I've got an ear for accents. They intrigue me.'

Sayid turned to find her eyes shadowed as if expecting disapproval. That was when he realised his jaw was locked tight and his hands bunched.

He nodded, curving his mouth into a smile and was pleased to see her tension ease. 'Part of your ear for languages, no doubt.' He turned to her coterie of admirers. 'Ms Rahman is fluent in several, you know.' Her teachers had been enthusiastic about her linguistic skills.

He stayed with the group, enjoying the lively change of pace from some of his more staid guests. Finally, when the others were deep in discussion, Lina turned to him. He looked down, seeing again that telltale twitch of concern on her brow.

'Lina?' He kept his voice low, below the level of the conversation surrounding them. 'What is it?'

'Have I done something wrong? You looked... angry earlier.'

It struck him that she alone had read his bad humour. Either he was slipping—he was adept at keeping his thoughts private—or she had an uncanny ability to read minds as well as accents. Neither idea appealed.

That was when he noticed her hands. Her posture was composed and she met his stare with her chin up, but her hands were clenched tight together.

To Sayid's surprise, that mix of pride and vulnerability tore at him. He should be pleased she held her own with this mixed group. Proud of her coping with a royal event. Many would find it intimidating.

'Not at all. You've done nothing wrong, Lina. On the contrary, it's good seeing you enjoying yourself.' He smiled down and watched as her expression grew dazzled.

Satisfaction, sweet, sharp and hot, spiked through him. A satisfaction he shouldn't feel but couldn't kill.

An hour after midnight, Lina leaned out over her balcony railing, staring beyond the capital to the vast starry sky. She inhaled the dry, slightly perfumed air of Halarq and felt a glow of excitement and happiness.

Sleep was beyond her. She felt like Cinderella after her ball. She'd attended a royal dinner party and instead of feeling out of place had met kind, interesting people. The conversation as much as the delicious food, the gold plate and crystal and the stunning setting made it a night to remember.

Especially when, before dinner, Sayid Badawi had stood beside her. In his robes, he'd been commanding yet urbane, charming yet with that tangible air of power. When his gleaming eyes rested on her she felt a quake of reaction like an earth tremor. At first she'd thought him angry, that she'd overstepped some rule of royal etiquette. But then he'd smiled…

Did he know how she came alive when he stood close? When he singled her out for conversation? How heat streaked through her, melting her, softening her body as if it ripened ready for his possession?

Perhaps he did for he hadn't lingered. Instead he'd borne off the friendly American to discuss trade.

Lina turned back into her room, pausing to soak up the atmosphere. Still she wasn't used to the suite's luxury. From the massive marble bathroom with its collection of fragrant bath oils beside the sunken tub to the lavishly appointed bedroom and sitting room, everything was exquisite. There were crystal perfume bottles, exquisite hand-woven carpets so thick you sank into them, and vases of fragrant roses, a rare delight in a desert kingdom.

Yet she couldn't settle. On impulse she marched to the dressing room where her belongings took up a tiny corner of the space. Quickly undressing, she put on her swimsuit and grabbed an oversized towel.

On one side her suite gave out onto a long, leafy courtyard that she hadn't explored. She'd been too busy with her new role, and too addicted to long soaks in the huge bath, to venture far. But she'd glimpsed a swimming pool at the far end.

Lina stepped barefoot onto warm flagstones. As always, there was no sign of life from the other rooms surrounding this garden. She was the only guest.

The sweet scent of jasmine filled her nostrils. Faint luminescence came from the stars and a myriad of tiny lights twining through the shrubs.

Lina smiled. It was a private fairyland.

She stepped into a patch of darker shade. Just ahead the underwater lights of the pool broke the darkness.

The soft aqua glow of the water beckoned enticingly. Lina was pulling pins from her hair, shaking the heavy tresses from her face, when a sound made her stop.

Splashing.

Not a fountain but the rhythmic slap of flesh cleaving through water.

Curious, Lina moved forward, peering between the shrubs. For a second she saw nothing but the ripple of light across the water. Then a dark head came into view, a long arm arcing out of the iridescent aqua and down again. Wide shoulders and a sinuous curve of spine. Another, tighter curve of flexing bare buttocks then long legs with a lazy kick that nevertheless propelled the tall body with enviable speed.

Lina sucked in a hiss of air, her hand belatedly slamming over her mouth to stop the sound. Dismayed, she stepped off the path, stumbling into a bush and snapping twigs.

There was only one person this could be. One person so at home in the palace that they'd swim here naked.

Only one person with those sublimely beautiful masculine proportions.

Somehow she'd blundered into Sayid Badawi's private garden!

She'd *known* there'd been a mistake when she was installed in those elegant rooms. More than once she'd thought the corridor leading to her suite was familiar from that night years ago when she'd sat by the Emir's bed. Till logic told her she imagined it. How could she remember one corridor from all those in this sprawling place?

Her heart hammered against her ribs and a chill

skipped down her spine. She couldn't let him find her here, invading his privacy.

Lina spun on her foot and stifled a gasp as something hard dug into her sole. She wasn't on the path any more. Worse, her long hair snagged on the bushes. Tiny twigs grabbed, refusing to release her.

She breathed slowly, tamping down panic as she fought to free herself. She couldn't hear splashing now, probably because her hammering pulse blotted out every other sound.

Finally, free of clinging plants, she got back on the path. She took a single step towards her rooms, then someone grabbed her upper arms and hauled her against a hard, dripping wet body.

CHAPTER FIVE

'WHO ARE YOU?' Sayid's voice was rough, every sense on alert.

He'd noticed movement in the shadows beyond the pool and instinct screamed a warning. Instinct that had, in the past, saved him more than once.

He'd swum to the end of the pool, vaulted out and prowled silently through the darkness to circle the silent watcher, approaching not from the lighted pool but the darkened garden.

A soft grunt of expelled air sounded as he hauled the intruder against him. An even softer body collided with his, a face against his chest, one smooth leg slipping against his.

What the—?

Swiftly he checked for weapons. Nothing. Just the extraordinary realisation that his intruder was female.

He peered down, making out the pale oval of an upturned face and a cascade of dark hair. Silky hair that draped over his chest and arm like a seductive blanket.

But it was the body against his that focused his thoughts. A curved, taut female body that seemed in the first instant of surprise to be unclothed. He moved a hand to her hip and found it covered in fabric that clung like a second skin. His fingers curved reflexively.

'You can let me go.' The voice, shaken but clear, came from near his collarbone.

Sayid identified that voice instantly. 'Lina? What are you doing here?'

He'd spent the evening trying to wrench his thoughts from the sight and sound of her, vibrant and beautiful in that clinging dress. Eventually he'd decided to work off his restlessness with exercise, only to find her, impossibly, here, in his private domain.

He breathed deep and felt the press of lush breasts against him. She was no schoolgirl any more. This was a woman, her body seductively ripe.

His body knew it. With her plastered against him and her breath feathering his nakedness, a weighted tension gathered in his loins. A clamouring rush of testosterone quickened his blood.

It had been months since his enjoyable interlude with that Danish actress. Now that seemed far too long ago.

'I didn't mean to intrude. I had no idea you were here. I thought the courtyard was deserted.' Was that panic in her voice? Fear?

Instantly Sayid stepped back, keeping his grip firm.

Air filled the gap between them but the sweet scent of her skin, like the fragrant damask roses his mother used to cultivate, lingered. As did Lina's warmth.

Desire, rough and urgent, slammed into him.

'Come into the light.' He led her towards the pool. Briefly it crossed his mind to clothe himself. But she'd already spied on his nakedness and it wasn't as if he had anything to hide. He was damned if he'd release his grip before he got an explanation.

There she stood, chin raised and eyes on a point near his shoulder, as he surveyed her in the glow of the underwater lights. It revealed every line and curve. From the sweet swell of her hips to her narrow waist and her high, lovely breasts. She'd been pressed against him and her one-piece swimsuit was wet. Wet enough to make her nipples peak. Which in turn increased the pressure in his groin.

He enjoyed beautiful women but kept a strict rein on his libido. Tonight his search for self-possession seemed futile. She'd filled his thoughts all evening and there was no escape even here, in his private space.

'Why are you spying on me?'

'I'm sorry. Truly.' Her eyes were huge as she met his stare and the crackle of energy between them detonated a silent explosion inside him. Yearning, desire...

She was pure seductress with that lush mouth and the shimmering dark hair falling to her waist. He should be furious at the invasion of privacy yet he wanted to comb his hand through her hair, enjoy the luxury of it against his skin. Not *think* but *feel*.

'I couldn't sleep and I knew there was a pool here.' The words tripped quickly from her lips. 'I thought a swim might help me relax. I had no idea...' She shook her head and that silky veil of hair slid across his hands where he held her. His flesh tightened. 'I didn't realise it was *your* pool. Then when I saw you—' she swallowed hard, her gaze slipping from his '—I planned to leave. But I got tangled in the bushes.'

'You didn't know this was my private wing?'

'Absolutely not!'

Her smooth brow wrinkled in obvious dismay.

Real or feigned?

The woman who'd returned to Halarq after years in Europe wasn't the same innocent who'd left. Lina was confident and beautiful, at ease with the adulation of men, as tonight had proved. But he couldn't quite believe she was like those predatory women who tried so hard to invade his privacy and his bed without invitation.

Yet she looked the picture of guilt. The question was whether it was because of an honest, though unlikely, mistake. Or simply because he'd caught her.

'You didn't seek me out?'

She gasped and shook her head, stiffening in his hold.

Once more her eyes met his and fire shot through his veins. He couldn't remember a more potent, instant response to any woman.

'Of course not. Why would I?'

Because you feel the throb of attraction between us too.

Because you want, as I do.

It was there in her convulsive swallow. In the fine tremors he felt running through her body. Not fear, he was certain, but arousal.

Sayid didn't say the words aloud. He retained, just, the sense to realise he was projecting his desires onto her.

Self-disgust smote him. Was he so needy? So desperate for a taste of those lips he, himself, had declared forbidden fruit?

'We'll discuss this in the morning.' Then, surely, he'd be able to think straight.

Stoically he ignored the seductive scent of her filling his nostrils.

Worse was the way she *looked* at him. Not like an embarrassed girl, but the way a woman looked at a man she desired.

It had to be unintentional. A trick of the light. Lina was, if no longer an innocent, at least not devious. She'd strayed here in error.

Yet now their gazes locked her nerves seemed to have disappeared. If anything she swayed ever so slightly towards him. Her gaze ate him up. Made him wonder exactly how much experience she'd acquired overseas, freed of the scrutiny of her family or any Halarqi supervision.

She was past the age when many women in his country became brides. No doubt there'd been plenty of foreign men ready to teach the little desert flower about love.

The notion brewed a bitter tang on his tongue.

Then Sayid registered the quick rise and fall of her breathing, the implicit invitation as she licked her lips and the faint, unmistakable fragrance of feminine arousal, mingling with her rose perfume.

He swallowed, stunned by the sudden certainty he wasn't the only one to *want*. He wasn't simply projecting his desires.

Yet Lina was his dependant, under his protection.

He was in a position of authority over her, with obligations as host, ruler and, above all, guardian. He couldn't act on his desire. He'd ensured that when he'd made her his ward.

Lina wasn't his to do with as he wished. She was no longer his concubine, provided for his pleasure.

But the memory of that night four years ago whispered through him, like a rain-laden wind rushing through a parched gully, promising an end to a long, painful drought. She'd offered herself then, ready to please his every whim.

'Lina! Don't look at me like that.' The words ground from him, harsh and ragged.

Again that quick swipe of her bottom lip, as if her mouth was as dry as his.

'Like what?' Still she didn't move away.

Sayid shook his head, determined to do the right thing as soon as he could unlock his hold on her arms.

Except she breathed deep and her breasts grazed him. A trail of fire rocketed through his ribs and abdomen, straight to his groin.

'Like you want me to kiss you.' He heard the rasp in his voice as duty battled desire, but she didn't respond to that harsh warning.

She blinked up at him, her lips parted and slowly shook her head, her hair caressing him. Then her words, soft as the flutter of a nightingale's wing, came to him. 'But I do.'

The night stood still, except for his heart slamming his ribs and the saw of his breath, loud in the silence. Yet, hard as he fought, control was beyond him now.

A moment later his mouth captured hers.

If she'd had the capacity to think properly Lina might have been astonished at how she'd spoken aloud, admitting her desire so blatantly.

Or by the way she responded to being locked against his hard form.

By the shivers of sensual delight she felt at the riot of new sensations.

This was outrageous, terrifying.

Wonderful.

Hard, callused hands grasped her tight. Sayid's warm breath feathered her face. His rich, potent scent swirled within her as if she'd absorbed his essence. And above all, the press of his wet, hard body against hers devastated her senses in the most thrilling way.

It was like a dream. Like those disturbing fantasies that had haunted her the last four years, growing ever bolder and more erotic.

Inevitably, as he bowed his head and possessed her mouth, Lina revelled in the fact this was no dream. She lifted her hands to his wet shoulders, relishing the strong bone, solid muscle and satiny skin beneath her questing hands.

Her daring surprised her, as if she made a habit of embracing men, when instead she'd spent years learning how to be friendly yet not encourage their advances.

Because, despite the stunning audacity of it, her heart, or perhaps her body, had fixed on Sayid Badawi as the only one she wanted. The one who, he'd made clear as he'd gently but firmly bundled her out of his bedroom and his life, was not for her. For of course he demanded sophistication and glamour, women who fitted his world of prestige and power.

This then was magic. A moment's aberration.

An opportunity not to be missed. For too soon reality would end it.

Lina fell into his embrace. So long she'd imagined his mouth on hers. So long she'd pined for his touch. There was no holding back, no hesitation. And she discovered her imagination was a poor imitation of the real thing.

Being held by Sayid, kissed by him, made her head spin and her heart pound in delight. The taste of him, so rich, so…intimate, made her weak at the knees. Lina would have been completely overwhelmed except that it felt *right*.

His powerful arms dragged her up so that her breasts were crushed against that imposing naked torso and she exulted in his strength, the urgency she sensed in him.

His lips were softer than she'd expected. But there was nothing tentative about his kiss. His tongue dived in, probing, licking and swirling. It invited hers to curl in a dance of give and take that made her body prickle with a searing heat despite her damp swimsuit.

She'd imagined sweet kisses. Had wondered about the open-mouthed kisses she'd seen in movies. But nothing, neither the excited chatter at school or the women's talk she'd heard in her old home, had prepared her for this.

If being near Sayid was like being bathed in starlight, this was like being tossed up into the bright Milky Way itself.

She slipped her hands higher, combing them through the drenched hair at the back of his skull, spreading her fingers and cupping his head possessively.

If she could, she'd hold him here for ever. Everyone knew magic was fleeting and she didn't want this to end.

His hand dragged up her side, almost but not quite touching her breast and she shuddered. A second later that large hand planted itself on her cheek, angling her head higher as he bowed her back across his arm.

That combination of tenderness and mastery undid her.

With a great thump of her heart Lina abandoned any attempt at thought and let herself go, knowing Sayid wouldn't let her fall. Everything his kiss demanded she gave, glorying not just in the delicious new physical sensations but her tangled, contrary feelings of power and helplessness.

When she pressed closer, sliding her tongue against his, he responded with a growl of pleasure deep in his throat that vibrated from his slick, hot body to hers. It made her quiver in delight.

She'd never felt so connected to another person. So…aroused. It was a heady new experience.

Liquid heat poured through her, pooling low in the centre of her body. Lina squirmed in his hold, trying to assuage the blind eagerness for more, more, more.

Then suddenly, devastatingly, it was over. Sayid's hands gripped her upper arms, holding her steady as he straightened away from her.

His broad bronzed chest rose and fell like overworked bellows. The furnace heat of his body encompassed her. But though she still tasted him on her tongue, her tingling lips couldn't reach him and her hands slipped from his head as he put her away from him.

Doubts assailed her. Regrets. Not for the kiss but because she hadn't wanted it to end.

Hadn't he enjoyed kissing her?

She was innocent but not that innocent. There'd been no mistaking his hard arousal between them. And that sound of pleasure he'd made, so low it rumbled through her bones—just remembering it made Lina shiver with luxurious pleasure.

Maybe she'd done it wrong. It was her first kiss, except for her cousin's clumsy attempt years ago. That didn't count, since his mouth had landed on her chin when she'd shoved him away.

Slowly Lina lifted her gaze, past the Emir's heaving pectorals with their fine covering of dark hair, past those hard, broad shoulders that had felt so strong beneath her hands. Even his throat looked powerful and sexy.

Lina blinked, realising she had a whole new appreciation of the meaning of the word. Sexy. That's what Sayid was. And his kiss sent her into orbit.

Steeling herself, she raised her eyes further. His mouth was a harsh line, set tight. If she couldn't still taste the rich flavour of him on her tongue, if her lips weren't swollen from his ardent kiss, she'd believe that mouth incapable of bestowing such bliss.

Lina wobbled, her legs unsteady, and instantly his hands firmed on her.

'Steady.' His voice was low, stroking places in her body she'd barely been aware of before now. She loved the differences between them. His size and strength were so much greater than hers. His experience too.

Finally she looked up to meet his blazing eyes. They were so dark they rivalled the black velvet sky behind him.

Whatever the reason for his withdrawal, it wasn't because he didn't want her.

An inner voice screamed that the issue wasn't just whether *he* wanted *her*. She had a say too. But that was a given, she acknowledged despairingly. No matter how often Lina told herself she was now an independent woman, she was utterly in thrall to His Royal Highness the Emir of Halarq.

'Are you all right?'

'Of course.' Lina struggled to keep her voice steady when inside all was turmoil. She'd dissolve into something perilously close to putty in those large hands should he kiss her again.

Sayid Badawi held part of her soul. He had from that first night, when she'd come to him, scared yet determined not to show it. Maybe it was gratitude that had turned into a teenage crush she hadn't grown out of. But whatever the reason, the compulsion she felt was real.

She desired the Emir.

Even now, with his mouth flat with disapproval, Lina wanted to kiss him again. And so much more.

Defiantly, ignoring the warning glitter in his gaze, she hiked her chin up. She wasn't ashamed of kissing him. He was a grown man, a powerful, experienced man. She hadn't forced him to kiss her.

'That was a mistake.' His low voice ground across her skin like sandpaper rasping tender flesh. 'It should never have happened.'

Lina opened her mouth to blurt out that it hadn't felt like a mistake. It had felt as close to perfect as anything she'd experienced in her life.

His expression snapped her mouth closed. She might disagree but clearly he felt differently.

For the first time since he'd kissed her, Lina felt

the hot sear of embarrassment. It branded her from her flaming cheeks to the soles of her feet and everywhere in between. Not because she'd responded with abandon, forgetting every lesson about modesty and morals. Not because there'd been nothing but the negligible barrier of her swimsuit between their naked bodies. But because, now he'd come to his senses, his distaste was obvious.

She was an orphaned charity case, a country-bred nobody who'd only just learned her letters. Who was she to think of kissing a prince?

She looked down, away from that haughty, beautiful face. But that gave her a view of the perfect symmetry of his collarbone, his masculine strength and—

'I'm sorry, Lina. That was my fault.'

Her head jerked up, eyes widening. 'No! It was mine.' She'd been the one incapable of hiding her desire. She'd urged him on, admitting she wanted his kiss. A fresh tide of heat engulfed her but Lina held his gaze. 'I'm sorry.'

It was a lie. She didn't regret any of it, except the moment he'd pulled away. And the troubled expression he wore now.

The forbidding lines clamping his mouth eased a little and his gaze warmed. 'Perhaps we could share the blame and agree it won't happen again.'

Belatedly Lina nodded, knowing it was another lie. One taste of his passion wasn't enough, but what option did she have but to agree? For a moment longer he regarded her in silence. She wished she knew what he was thinking. But on second thoughts, it was probably better not to know.

Words formed on her lips, a tumble of emotional, desperate words that would only betray her feelings and embarrass him. Resolute, she kept her mouth closed.

'Wait here.' He released her and swung away.

Instantly she missed his warmth, his support. She even found herself stumbling a fraction, she who'd inherited her mother's grace and balance.

Lina told herself not to but her gaze followed him as he strode around the pool. Completely naked, his back view was one of the most enthralling sights she'd witnessed. Far more fascinating than the glaciers and remorseless mountain peaks that had captivated her in Switzerland. The curve of the spine that ended in the strong, bunching muscles of his glutes. The breadth of his shoulders compared with his narrow hips. The long, strong legs that—

He grabbed a towel and swung round, whipping the fabric around his hips as he turned. Immediately Lina blinked and averted her stare, pretending fascination with the aqua luminescence of the pool.

'How did you know about the pool?' It took a second or two to clear her head and focus on the words.

'Pardon?'

He stood before her now, arms crossed over a chest that was definitely heavier and broader than it had been four and a half years ago. The sight of him sent another judder of appreciation right to her core.

'The pool, Lina. How did you know where to find it?'

Lina ripped her attention away from his body. Was it always like this when a woman desired a man? She'd had no idea such feelings could addle the brain.

'I caught a glimpse from my rooms, but I didn't—'

'Your rooms?' He didn't sound angry. His voice wasn't much above a whisper, yet she sensed something wrong.

She nodded. Of course her suite was a mistake, too grand for her. It was probably meant for some visiting ambassador and there'd been a horrible mix-up.

But not hers. She'd done nothing wrong. *Except throw yourself at the royal ruler of the kingdom.*

'Down there.' She waved a hand towards the far end of the courtyard. 'You can just see a patch of water through the plants. I thought this wing was deserted, you see. I'd never noticed any lights but mine.'

'You'd better show me.' Again his voice was even and well-modulated. Yet Lina knew he wasn't happy.

Sayid followed her along the path. She paused where they'd grappled, bending to retrieve a towel she'd dropped.

His eyes had adjusted to the semi-darkness and nothing could have prevented his gaze following her movement, zeroing in on that peach-perfect backside so lovingly moulded by her swimsuit.

Heat sluiced his body as desire flamed red-hot.

He knew lust of old. Had learned to manage it, giving in to it only for short stints. But this… He shook his head. This was unprecedented.

He'd swear Lina didn't know how provocative that movement was. Or that the sway of her hips as she walked was pure invitation.

Her supple movements as much as the delicious shape of her body ratcheted up his tension, and his arousal. Too easily he imagined himself entwined with Lina, her legs around him, pulling him to her with the raw enthusiasm she'd exhibited when they kissed. She'd be a passionate lover and he wanted her badly. He actually shook with the effort it took not to give in and haul her against him, under him and—

Lina stopped. Sayid realised she was at the door to the main guest suite.

It wasn't one of the regular suites. This was re-served for the Emir's most intimate friends. Part of his private apartments, it was set aside for his lover of the moment.

'Who let you in here?'

Her forehead crinkled at the bark in his voice but she didn't shrink back. 'Your chamberlain. Is there a problem? I thought it a mistake. I didn't expect to be in such luxurious rooms.' Her hands tightened on the towel she held. 'I'll pack up now and—'

'No. There's no need.'

And no point. The damage was done. By now it would be common knowledge to anyone who cared to find out that Lina had spent each night apparently at his beck and call.

It made no difference that nothing had happened between them. Except for that incendiary kiss. What mattered was that Lina had moved into the rooms reserved for his short-term lovers. Moving her out now would achieve nothing but speculation that he'd grown tired of her.

Sayid rubbed a hand over his tight jaw. The very thing he'd sought to protect her from, or at least part of it, had happened despite his good intentions.

Many of his uncle's staff had been replaced in the last few years, but obviously someone in the palace remembered Lina's arrival as a personal gift to the Emir. The expectation that she'd become his concubine. They must have informed the chamberlain, who'd assumed Sayid would want his lover near.

What a hellish mess.

Yet as he thought it, part of him, the ruthless part ready to snatch what he wanted and hold it by force if necessary, revelled in having her so conveniently close.

All he had to do was reach out and take her.

Anticipation skated over his skin as he looked down at her ripe lips. Her kiss had been delightfully enthusiastic.

'Sir? Is there a problem?'

It was the *Sir* that stopped him. The reminder that far from being equals, all the power rested with him. She deferred to him, obeyed him.

Who knew what she'd do out of obedience?

Bile rose in his throat. He'd never forced a woman in his life.

Guilt spiralled through his belly, rising to clog his chest. It was one thing to invite a sophisticated foreign woman to become his short-term lover. It was another to seduce his own ward! The woman he'd gone to such lengths to protect. The woman who, even with the gloss of recent foreign experience, was indebted to him and who, he knew, took debts of honour seriously. Look at the way she'd held back on accepting the education she so desired, till he'd found a way for her to pay him back.

It was unthinkable that Lina Rahman should give him lessons in honour. And yet...

Sayid remembered his youthful disdain for his un-

cle's sybaritic lifestyle. For the unbridled self-indulgence and licentiousness. Yet when Sayid had scoffed
about him being a roué, his father had opened his eyes
to Sayid's own weaknesses.

There was a strong streak of sensuality and self-
indulgence in the family, he'd said. Down the generations they had a reputation for being passionate
and hot-blooded, overstepping the bounds. That made
them formidable warriors, greedy for victory and its
spoils. But there was a constant need to rein in that
tendency. The blood flowing through Sayid's uncle
flowed in their veins too. And the potential to wallow
in selfish pleasure. It was Sayid's duty, he'd said, to
be strong and honourable. To put responsibility above
pleasure and resist corruption.

'No. There's no problem.' Sayid made himself step
back from the door. 'It's late. You should turn in. It's
been a long evening.' He swung away from the door
then stopped.

Slowly he turned back, reading tension in her slim
form. See? He'd done right, putting her away from
him.

Yet still he lingered.

'Don't call me sir.' Logic told him he was mad,
smashing that barrier of formality. Yet he felt sick
when Lina used his title. As if she'd kissed him because of his position, his authority over her. The idea
was untenable.

'But I…' Her eyes rounded. 'You're the Emir.'

As if he could forget. If he weren't, if he were simply a man who'd met a beautiful young woman, it
would be so much easier to deal with the feelings
Lina stirred.

'I think we've got beyond that, don't you?' It was hard to tell in the shadows but he'd swear she blushed. 'As my ward—' he bit back a grimace on the word '—you have the right to call me by name.'

He didn't have a clue what the protocol was. Yet he knew a sudden, fierce urge to have this from Lina at least, since honour dictated he could have no more. The sound of his name on her tongue.

'And I would prefer it.'

Her chin hiked higher, her eyes meeting his with that same unabashed stare he'd noticed the day she'd returned to Halarq. An electric charge sparked in the air between them.

'As you wish—' she paused so long he found himself leaning towards her in anticipation '—Sayid.'

Her voice was like a sighing night breeze, wafting the scent of spices and sweetness. It was a voice that would haunt him through the long sleepless hours of the night.

Abruptly he nodded, then turned and stalked away down the path to his suite. He didn't look back. It was only wishful thinking that tried to convince him Lina stood, watching every step.

Four years ago she'd sorely tested his willpower as he battled the urge to claim her. Incredibly he faced the same problem again. The urge to reach out and simply grab what he wanted. With Lina he had no off switch.

Sayid breathed in the garden's honeysuckle perfume. Yet another scent lingered, teasing, in his nostrils. The scent of roses and female flesh.

He set his jaw, ignoring the memory of that sexy body flush against his.

It was going to be a long night. But he vowed by the end of it he'd have a solution to the taunting, seductive problem that was Lina, distracting him from his work, and the dictates of honour.

CHAPTER SIX

SAYID WAS IMPRESSED as the group of local elders showed him through the community centre he'd funded. He'd heard good reports of it, including last night from his Minister for Education, who'd visited as part of his programme to increase school attendance.

With Lina, he recalled.

They'd all liked Lina.

Sayid's mouth firmed as he realised she'd slipped into his thoughts again. All night she'd been on his mind, since that mind-numbing kiss.

Finally, in the early hours, he'd come up with a solution to her distracting presence. It would mean never seeing her again, forcing her to get on with her own life far from him. Resolutely he ignored the inner silent howl of outrage at being deprived of her. It was for the best.

'Would Your Highness be interested in seeing the final space?' His guide indicated doors at the end of the room.

A grey-bearded elder spoke. 'It would probably not be of interest, sire. It's only where the women gather.' His expression and tone were dismissive. Exactly the attitude Sayid and his reformist staff had worked so hard to change.

'I'd be pleased to see what use they make of it. If our presence won't disturb them.' Traditionally women stayed apart from men.

The first man nodded. 'It is good of Your Highness to ask. But there can be no objection.' Nevertheless, he nodded to his grandson, who accompanied them. The boy ran off to warn the matrons of the visit. He slipped through the door and Sayid heard laughter, clapping and singing.

Obviously the women were having far more fun than the men this morning.

Intrigued, Sayid followed his guide to the double doors that opened onto a wide courtyard surrounded by colonnades. Fig and pistachio trees shaded the yard and at the centre of the far wall, surrounded by tiles of blue and aqua, a fountain streamed into a shallow pool.

The aroma of new bread hung in the air, and the rich melding of scents, rose, jasmine and lily, from the group of women seated all around the space.

All this he absorbed in moments, but it was the movement at the centre of the courtyard that caught his attention. Amidst the smiling, singing group, three young women danced, their long skirts billowing around them. One wore the traditional necklaces and headscarf of a bride and sunlight glinted off flashing antique silver coins as she turned.

But it was another dancer who held Sayid's gaze. Ebony tresses drifted around her shoulders, all the way to her tiny waist, as she circled. Her hands described a series of intricate, elegant shapes as she twirled, every movement, every dip and sway, graceful.

Lina. His heart slammed into his ribs then took up an uneven beat.

She wore a long traditional dress of russet red, unadorned but for a scarf of red and lilac belted at her waist, the ends flaring out as she spun. Her dress was less elaborate than the ones worn by the others but his eyes were drawn to her as inevitably as one of his Bedouin ancestors spying a life-giving oasis in the desert.

Pleasure swelled at the sight of her, nimble, supple and beautiful. There was desire—that was inevitable with Lina—but there was more too, the appreciation of any bystander watching a master at work. She could have been a professional dancer with those exquisitely light movements that looked deceptively easy but which he knew took years and considerable skill to perfect.

'Your Highness.' His guide spoke. 'Allow me to introduce my wife and my wife's sister.'

Sayid dragged his attention back to the introductions, smiling and making small talk with the group of older women who'd come to greet him.

'My granddaughter is to be married soon and the girls are practising the dances for the celebration,' one woman explained.

Just then there was a shout of laughter and another of warning. Sayid turned to see a little girl, who'd been trying to emulate the dancers, twirl too fast and lose her balance, running full tilt into Lina. A second little girl, presumably trying to catch her friend, raced after her but, dizzy from the spinning, toppled against her instead.

There was a flurry of skirts and Lina, with her two small assailants, tumbled to the ground.

The singing stopped, the other dancers whirling to a halt.

Then, breaking the silence, came the husky sound of laughter. It was joyous and uninhibited. Contagious too, especially when Lina's face emerged from the tumble of bodies, wearing a grin as bright as the sun. Her laughter was like that too, bright and glorious.

It struck Sayid that he'd missed the sound of laughter these last years as he strove full-time to do his duty for his country.

As he watched, Lina reached for one little girl, tickling her. Then the sounds of mirth filled the courtyard as the two little girls squealed in mock dismay, pretending, but not too hard, to escape.

Lina's hair was in her eyes and she was gasping as her two small tormentors tickled her, when a low rumbling sound caught her ears. Rich and mellow, warm and inviting, the male laughter tugged at something inside. She lifted her head, intrigued, brushing a swathe of hair back from her face.

One of the children took that as a cue to burrow closer and Lina automatically wrapped an arm around her. This pair was a delight and for some reason had shadowed Lina since she'd arrived.

Struggling up, she propped herself on her other hand and almost fell back to the floor. For standing near the courtyard entrance, at least a head taller than those around him, was the Emir, resplendent in white robes.

Sayid. The name whispered through her brain and

she recalled the sound of it on her tongue, the delicious, dangerous taste of it as she'd called him that last night. Had she imagined that flare of desire in his eyes in response?

She didn't know what to think. Logic said he'd wanted her, yet he'd put her aside easily.

Lina had told herself it was for the best. That kiss had been dangerous. But now cautious Lina was silent. Since last night a needy, yearning woman had taken her place. Her fixation on the man who'd turned her life around had morphed from a crush into full-blown infatuation.

She wanted Sayid. Never so much as now, hearing that lush, glorious laugh, seeing his face crease into a grin of simple amusement.

He'd never looked so devastatingly handsome. So young and approachable. As if she could go over there and speak to him as an equal. Lift her hand to that thick, soft dark hair covering his scalp and pull his head down to hers. She'd stand on tiptoe and lift her mouth to his and—

The laughter stopped as his eyes met hers.

There was a crack of instant, explosive tension she was surprised no one else seemed to hear. Suddenly her heart was racing faster than it had as she'd danced, and a fine film of heat glazed her skin from head to toe. One look, one smile, and she was undone. Even after last night's rejection. Hot blood flooded her cheeks.

What was he doing here?

Why was he looking at her that way when he'd made it clear he was out of bounds after that kiss? He didn't just look. His gaze *devoured*.

A second later the heat blazing in his eyes was banked and he turned to the older group surrounding him, saying something that made them nod.

Of course, he wasn't here looking for her. What a stupid fantasy! He was here because he'd championed this centre and his staff were trying to convince people to send all their children to the new school nearby. Because the Emir believed it better for his people to *want* education than to force them.

Sayid was totally unlike his uncle. Parents had scared their children with stories of the previous Emir, a bogeyman who'd come to get them if they didn't behave.

Sayid was no bogeyman but he drove her crazy, she decided as she got up and righted her two little companions. His position meant she couldn't pursue her attraction—he'd made that clear as he put her aside last night and the memory stabbed her heart. Yet she couldn't leave while she was obliged to him. She was caught like a moth, dazzled by flame. All she could do was endure.

For ninety minutes she was on her best behaviour, co-opted into the royal party as he finished his tour then entered the old souk, pausing here and there to talk to stallholders and shoppers alike. There were a couple of discreet guards but they hung back so there was no obvious barrier between Sayid and his people.

Again Lina was fascinated by what she saw. Not a man caught up in his own importance, but one who'd happily sample dates from the clawed hand of an ancient stallholder, who chatted easily with businesspeople and passers-by clustering around.

Nor was it just his ease that impressed her. It was

the questions he asked and the way he listened. More than once Lina saw him nod to his secretary to take a note of a matter to be followed up. The walk-through wasn't for show. His interest was genuine.

Lina admired Sayid, too much. Everything she learned confirmed her first impression, that he was a man worthy of respect. The trouble was, she felt far more than respect, which was why, on entering the citadel, she made to hurry to her room.

'Not so fast, Lina. We have matters to discuss.'

He didn't put out a hand to prevent her leaving, but that tone, with its ring of authority, stopped her in her tracks. This was her ruler, not the hungry man she'd clung to last night. The one who'd tasted of dark, sensual secrets she longed to learn.

Her nape prickled and suddenly her chest was too tight, as if her lungs had swollen and there was no room to breathe.

'This way.' He led her through grand reception rooms, past the throne room, thank goodness. Standing before him there on her first day back as he sat high on the royal dais had been one of the most daunting things she'd done.

He opened a door and Lina stepped into a book-lined room, splendid yet welcoming. The room where he'd promised to send her to school. Her gaze darted to the shelf of books she'd been unable to read all those years ago.

Pride stirred. She still preferred the spoken word to the written, but she'd worked hard to become literate.

Was he proud of what she'd achieved? He'd never said. Lina told herself it didn't matter. She'd done it for herself, not him.

'Take a seat.'

Obediently she sat, only to find Sayid had planted himself in the centre of the room, feet wide and hands clasped behind his back. His stance projected power and authority, yet the line of his jaw and the set of his shoulders gave the impression of tension.

Memory flashed, of his taut body against hers as he kissed her senseless. But *she* was the one on edge because of that. He'd taken it in his stride.

'I've been thinking about your future, Lina. You can't stay here indefinitely.'

It was what Lina had wanted—to get on with her life. Yet, rather than rejoicing, pain tore through her. She wasn't ready to leave him. Especially after last night. It had been like opening a door and stepping into a whole new glorious world. She felt *transformed* by what she'd experienced in Sayid's arms.

Pride and sense came to her rescue. 'Of course not.'

He nodded, yet his dark eyebrows angled down in the centre of his forehead as if he were displeased. Lina kept her gaze on him. He'd been as much a party to what happened last night as she—more so, given her lack of experience. She refused to feel guilty.

'I'm glad you agree.' His mouth curved up at the edges, but it wasn't a real smile, not like she'd seen earlier this morning. 'Which is why I've decided it's time to find you a husband.'

Lina's mouth dropped open. Her eyes popped. Her entire body froze, except her fingers clawing at her chair for support.

Finally, as hurt filled her chest and her vision misted, she remembered to breathe, her lungs heaving, dragging in oxygen. Even then, she felt like she had on that first ever flight, the day she'd left Halarq. As the ground had dropped and the jet had vibrated and dipped before rising into the sky, there was a moment when she'd seemed completely cut off from every reality she'd ever known.

'Husband?' Her voice wasn't her own and she licked her lips, trying to moisten them.

Sayid's gaze flicked to her mouth then away. Abruptly he moved to take a seat across from her. 'Most Halarqi women your age are married.'

Lina slumped back in her chair, hefting another breath. He wanted her married and out of his hair.

Why not? Did you think he wants a starry-eyed ward under his feet?

It's not as if you're his type. Last night proved that, no matter how wonderful it felt to you.

Logic told Lina it was ridiculous to be hurt that Sayid wanted to see her, not just out of his palace, but shackled to another man. Yet that didn't stop the deep-seated ache flooding through her.

How could she *think* about another man when being in the same room as Sayid made her heart race and her body tense with desire?

The notion of kissing another man as she'd kissed Sayid last night, of doing *more*, made her nauseous.

A lump of cold dread settled in her belly.

'Since you left your uncle's house, I'm responsible for you. I'll do my best to find you a husband you'll find agreeable.'

Lina blinked, wondering if perhaps she'd hit her head when she'd fallen while dancing with the children. Was there a chance this was a dream?

But this was real. From the stiff back of the gilded

chair behind her to the rich carpet underfoot and the distinctive scent of the room—old books and the merest hint of citrus and cedar wood. Sayid's room, more so than the lavish reception rooms where he made his public appearances.

'*You'll* choose a husband for me?' Her voice was croaky but at least it worked.

'My staff will assist, but as your guardian I'll approve the final choice.'

Lina shook her head. He made it sound as if there were hordes of men waiting to be yoked to a woman whose own family had disowned her and whose guardian had never wanted her, even when she'd all but begged for his attention. She didn't belong anywhere and had nothing to recommend her but a nice face, a talent for languages and some skill at dressmaking.

And as if she wanted a husband.

'I'll have them draw up a list.' Sayid's voice was clipped. He wanted this over. 'But if there's anything or any*one* in particular they should consider, now is the time to tell—'

'No.' Lina hadn't consciously formed the word, but sucked in a breath of relief when it stopped his speech.

'Sorry?' Sayid's gaze moved from its focus somewhere across the room to zero in on her face. Lina felt the weight of his stare as surely as a touch. 'You're saying you don't have any suggestions? No likes or dislikes?'

She shook her head, wishing she hadn't left her hair loose when she went to visit the women this morning. Looking into those dark eyes, and not revealing her desperate longings, took courage. Wearing her hair up would have made her feel less of a country bumpkin before this powerful man in his grand palace.

'I mean I don't want to get married.'

Lina saw the flare of disbelief in Sayid's eyes and hurriedly sat straighter, crossing her ankles and composing her hands in her lap as her mother had taught her. 'Thank you... *Sayid*.' She breathed carefully, willing down the riot of see-sawing emotions. 'I appreciate your good intentions, but I don't want a husband.'

'Don't *want* a husband?' His tone was one of disbelief. Halarqi girls were brought up to think of marriage and babies as their twin goals in life. She even thought she heard an echo of her aunt's outrage just before she'd harangued Lina about one of her many failings. It was a tone that didn't invite a response.

Yet Lina couldn't let this slide. In the beginning she'd been awed by the Emir's authority and more lately by knowledge of the debt she owed him. And by her own response to him as a man. But this was her life! She simply couldn't stay silent.

'No, thank you. It's very kind of you to bother on my behalf but—'

'It's my wish to see you settled with a husband.' His tone, though even, was that of a man used to having his every whim obeyed. Here was a reminder that despite his generosity, and the decadent magic of his kiss, Sayid was absolute ruler to millions.

She ducked her head, her mind racing for a solution that wasn't outright opposition.

'That's very gracious of you, and I do appreciate it, but I have no intention of marrying.'

Not till I've got you out of my system.

To marry another man while her heart and body yearned for this one would be impossible.

There was a flurry of robes as the Emir rose. He turned to pace first towards her then away, to the massive desk piled with folders and papers.

'You don't *intend* to marry.' Anger threaded his words. 'Why? Because it doesn't suit you?' He swung round and glared at her, pinioning her to the chair.

'I'm sorry. I—'

'Is this to do with what happened last night? If so let me be clear. You can't expect—'

'I expect nothing!' Lina shot to her feet, her hands clenched fists at her sides.

Wasn't it enough that he'd pushed her away then told her that magical kiss had been a *mistake*?

'I know you don't want me. I know that kiss was my fault.' For she'd been the one pleading with her eyes, the one who'd told him she wanted him. She might not have a lot of personal experience but she understood enough to know that men weren't always discriminating if women threw themselves at them. He hadn't really wanted *her*.

Lina pushed her shoulders back, glaring at him, for the first time not caring about his power or authority. Seeing only the man she wanted, rejecting her yet again.

Her lips crumpled in a derisive smile. First her uncle and aunt had packed her off. Then Sayid. Now he was doing it again. Hopefully one day she'd find someone who *wanted* her to stay, who didn't see her simply as an unwanted burden.

Furious tears gathered at the back of her eyes and

she blinked, hating the possibility he'd think she felt sorry for herself.

On the contrary, she was proud. She'd worked hard to make something of herself and one day she'd be a brilliant interpreter, in great demand. She'd support herself with her work and have a home and friends. One day she might even fall in love with a man who loved her back.

'The simple fact is I don't want a husband. And if ever I do I'll choose him myself. Thank you.'

He looked down at her with a hauteur she'd never seen in him before. Like a warrior of old confronted with a disobedient slave. Lina swallowed and stood her ground, even as he stepped close enough to loom over her.

She wasn't a slave any more. He'd released her from that.

Sayid stared down into Lina's flushed, vibrant face and forced his clenched hands behind his back. All morning he'd been hyper-aware of her, even as he'd conducted his tour, talking with scores of others. She'd stood silent, a little behind him, but he'd breathed in her light floral scent, been conscious of the stares of others, taking in her beauty. More than once, on turning, his breath had clogged in his lungs as he'd seen her and fought to resist the urge to grab the soft length of her hair, wrap it round his hand and tug her hard against him. He wanted to taste her again, experience the heady combustion of desire when they came together.

But he couldn't, damn it…because he was doing the decent thing.

And did she thank him for it?

He looked down into flashing violet eyes, the ripe mouth, set in mulish lines, and wondered why even her mutinous attitude was too attractive.

Because he was tired of people deferring?

Or because her fire reminded him of how she'd felt in his arms?

'While I appreciate your concern for me, it's unnecessary.' Her eyes locked with his, no hint of backing down. 'Halarq is changing. You've said it's good for women to have careers now. That's what I want.'

Damn her! She had the temerity to quote his own words back at him.

Sayid ground his molars, surprised to discover that while he despised yes-men, he wasn't keen on disobedience either. 'There's no reason you can't have both a husband and a career.'

'But I'm not ready for a husband. I want to—'

'You're my responsibility. I'll decide what's best for you.'

Her head rocked back as if she'd been slapped. Yet he'd said nothing untoward. He had an obligation to see to her security and welfare.

'I'm twenty-two. Old enough to make decisions about my future.'

She had a point. He'd been treated as an adult since he was fifteen. But then his circumstances were different.

'Enough!' Sayid rounded the desk and sat down, occupying the position of power as she stood before him. 'You can trust me to find you a decent man.'

Instead of reassuring her, his words seemed to detonate her intriguingly volatile temper. He'd had hints of it in the past, like when she'd described her undesirable cousins and when she'd boldly met his gaze when so many wouldn't. Yet he'd had no notion she could be so easily provoked, except in passion. The knowledge was disturbingly…arousing.

She planted her hands on her hips and her eyes flashed amethyst fire. Her cheeks were rose pink, her lips the colour of mountain cherries.

She looked…incendiary and captivatingly sensual.

'When I want a man I'll find him for myself, thank you very much.' Her chin tipped up. 'For all your talk of modernisation and rights for the disenfranchised, you don't believe your own rhetoric, do you? You still see women as possessions, unable to make decisions for themselves.'

Sayid was on his feet in a second, palms flat on his desk as he leaned across it towards her. 'Nothing could be further from the truth.'

'Then prove it. Don't dictate to me.'

'In case you've forgotten, Lina, I'm your guardian. It's my job to make decisions for you.'

If he'd thought his anger would make her back down, he was mistaken. She paled, but instead of subsiding, she paced right up to the other side of his desk, holding his gaze with all the calm composure of a born leader.

Her perfume teased his nostrils. That rich rose scent took him straight back to last night, when the taste of her sweet mouth and the torture of her body against his had driven him to the brink of madness. He'd almost taken her right there on the hard flagstones by the pool.

He shook his head, trying to clear the miasma of desire enveloping him.

'Damn it, Lina. You'll do as you're told!'

She didn't even flinch. Instead she planted her own palms on the desk and leaned into his personal space, as no one else would dare.

'Are you saying you'd *force* me?' She heaved a breath that made her lush breasts swell against the fitted bodice of her red dress. 'Are we returning to the days when women were chattels to be bartered between men? I thought you objected to that. Or was all that just fine words?'

Sayid reared back, stunned and furious. Lina couldn't have got it more wrong. He knew the ugly reality of life for women under his uncle's outdated regime.

At fifteen Sayid had been all that stood between his beautiful widowed mother and rape then a forced marriage to one of his uncle's cronies. Rape then a quick wedding being an easy way to acquire a widow's wealth.

Sayid had stood up to the man his mother had rejected, sword in hand, and fought for her right to choose. He'd fought for his own life too, for her disgruntled suitor had no qualms about killing those who got in his way.

The ancient knife slash up Sayid's arm throbbed with a phantom pain at the memory.

'You *dare* to question my morals? This is the thanks I receive after all I've done for you?'

Lina's ingratitude stung. Yet at the same time Sayid felt something more. A quickening of dark excitement as she stood up to him.

Heat bloomed anew in her pale face, dark red flagging her high cheekbones. Yet still she didn't back down. Either she'd completely forgotten whom she was talking to or she was more recklessly courageous than any adult male in the country. For none would meet him head-on like this.

'You want my *gratitude*?' She almost spat the word at him. 'You have it. You've had it for over four years. Why do you think I worked so hard at that school, even in the beginning when it was pure torment? Why do you think I stuck it out? To prove your faith in me was justified. That I wouldn't let you down. Day after day I ignored the ridicule and teasing, the fear that maybe I didn't have it in me to succeed. Because I wanted you to be proud of me.'

Sayid frowned. This was the first he'd heard of ridicule or teasing. Surely he'd have been informed—

'Not that you were interested. I never heard from you, not once in all that time.' She hefted a quick breath that did something strange to his internal organs. 'But that didn't matter. I kept at it because I was grateful, and because *I* wanted an education. I'm working with your educators to pay off the debt I owe you, because I'm grateful and—'

'Enough!' Sayid put up his hand, horrified at the undercurrent of emotions her words evoked. Emotions he couldn't, didn't want to name, but which left him raw and weakened. As if someone had taken a sword to his knees, cutting off the strength in his limbs. 'There is no debt. You're free to leave.'

'With a husband you choose for me?' She shook her head so violently her ebony hair swung wide, brushing his upraised hand, drawing his body to instant arousal.

Instantly he was back in the courtyard last night, that silky weight caressing his bare skin as he drove his tongue into her mouth, going mad on the taste and feel of her. On the untrammelled hunger he'd never be able to sate.

'No, thank you.' She was as proud as an empress, looking down her nose at him, even from her inferior height. 'I'll work off my debt as agreed. In the position you created to appease my pride.' He must have started because she nodded. 'Even I can see you don't need me when you've got trained professionals to do the job. But I'll stick at it because I'm *grateful* and I pay back my debts.'

Fleetingly he thought of telling her those professionals thought she was more effective than the rest of them put together. But that could wait.

Sayid didn't know if it was the sniping way she said she was grateful, or the thought of her staying in the palace for months, possibly years, till her conscience told her she'd paid off the debt of her education.

Maybe it was the flare of unfamiliar recklessness engendered by her jabs at his conscience.

Or the heady rush of adrenaline from being so close to Lina when she forgot herself and transformed into this magnificent, proud, indomitable, *desirable* woman.

Suddenly all the leashes, the checks and stays Sayid had placed on his baser impulses snapped. There was a roaring in his ears, a feeling of release as he leaned across the desk so his words feathered her lips.

'If you're so determined to pay back your debt to me, Lina, there's a much better way.'

He saw her eyes widen, a flare of brilliant violet alive with...trepidation or excitement?

There was one way to find out.

'Come to my bed. Be my lover for a week and the debt is cancelled.'

CHAPTER SEVEN

SILENCE THUNDERED BETWEEN THEM. A bold, heavy silence that throbbed with the beat of his blood and the sound of her indrawn breath.

Sayid waited for shame to engulf him at his outrageous, inexcusable suggestion. But it didn't come. Instead there was relief at finally conceding his need for her, despite the dictates of honour and obligation.

Of course, she'd be horribly embarrassed by his proposition.

Yet Lina didn't look away. Nor did she move back, though he'd thrust his head so close to hers he was just about in kissing distance. All he had to do was wrap his hand around the nape of her neck and tug.

Would she resist? Would she curse and spit and claw at his face?

Not this woman, he realised.

Not when her eyes blazed with surprise. And could it be? A hint of curiosity?

Not a smidgen of outrage in sight. No embarrassment or shyness.

Lina stared back at him, lips slightly parted as if she couldn't pull in enough oxygen, breasts rising and falling with each rapid breath, with her face still upturned to his.

Not like a supplicant or a charity case.

Why had he ever thought her shy? Because in the past she'd ducked her head and called him by his title, deferring to him? But of course she'd do that. He was her ruler. Her whole future depended on him. Hadn't he been fascinated by the flashes he'd seen of her spirit, like when she'd refused to accept his charity unless she could repay him?

Then there was the way she told you she wanted you to kiss her.

She looked at him with the bright, steady gaze of a woman considering his words, assessing him as an equal.

He liked it, he realised with a blast of exhilaration.

Her tongue slipped out to moisten her lower lip and Sayid's belly clenched. Yet he'd swear the action wasn't intentional flirtation, not now her forehead puckered in confusion.

'Why only a week?'

Of all the things she might have said, Lina chose merely to query his time limit?

What a woman! Sayid admired her forthrightness, her lack of coyness. And, of course, the fact she hadn't instantly dismissed his proposal.

He'd thrown out the proposition because he'd reached the end of his patience. And he admitted darkly, just possibly to frighten her into submission. But it seemed she was actually considering it.

Savagely he repressed a smile, knowing it would surely reveal his rapaciousness. Lina had sorely tested him and now, with the echo of his proposition hanging in the air between them, it was hard to claw back even a fraction of the self-denial he'd worked hard to maintain.

'I only take lovers for a week. That's all the time I can spare.' Having a self-imposed deadline ensured he'd return his focus to his official responsibilities and not be tempted into a life of sybaritic luxury like his uncle.

To his amazement, Lina's lips twitched. Was that a hint of amusement dancing in her eyes? What had happened to the virago who taunted and obstructed him?

'Because you're in such demand?'

Sayid felt a smile tug at the corners of his mouth, until she lifted her hands from the desk and straightened. Instantly he missed her nearness, but he resisted the impulse to stalk around the desk and crowd her.

He was too proud to try to coerce her. Wasn't he?

'Because I believe in setting limits. Pleasure can become a weakness if it's uncontrolled.'

Slowly she nodded. 'I see. Plus of course you wouldn't want any woman getting ideas of permanency.'

It was true, but that had never been a problem. Once he'd had his week with a woman she was sent off with a fond farewell and enough lavish gifts to sweeten the parting.

Sayid didn't bother to mention that his women were usually foreigners, more ready to accept a week of luxury and erotic pleasure for what it was—mutual enjoyment with no strings attached. It struck him that Lina's attitude reflected the years she'd lived away from Halarq. Most Halarqi women would expect marriage before sex. But she took this proposition in her stride. It seemed her mores were more western than Halarqi now. No doubt she'd sampled those western freedoms. That probably explained too her unwillingness to marry.

He was torn between pleasure that she'd been more amenable to his suggestion and a stirring of vague discontent at the idea of her with other men. Even the notion of her leaving the palace and settling down some time in the future with a worthy husband was strangely disquieting.

Sayid yanked his straying thoughts back in line.

'You're not saying anything.' The lengthening silence goaded him. He was used to women falling over themselves to please him. Firmly he repressed the voice of his conscience protesting that what he asked was scandalous and indecent—taking advantage of a woman under his protection.

Yet the situation wasn't so simple. It was clear Sayid had to re-evaluate Lina. Yes, she was under his protection, but she wasn't afraid to stand up to him and speak her mind.

'I'm surprised.' For a second she looked away and he wondered if, after all, he was wrong. Was she distressed? Then she slanted her gaze in his direction and he felt that bone-deep sizzle of sensual connection. 'I didn't think you wanted me like that.'

'Even after last night?' It seemed impossible.

She shrugged, yet he had the impression she wasn't as composed as before. 'Men respond to certain stimuli. We were almost naked and I told you I wanted you to kiss me.' She paused and made a production of pushing her hair back over her shoulders. 'I assumed it was more to do with the moment than me.'

Sayid crossed his arms over his chest and felt the pound of his heart, heavy and quick. Thinking about that embrace had occupied most of the night, in between devising a scheme to get Lina out of the palace.

Now he decided the palace was exactly the place for her. Specifically in his bed.

'You assumed wrong.' His voice dropped to a rough note that made her start. Had he frightened her? She might be experienced but Sayid was a man of strong passions and right now they simmered close to the surface.

Lina tilted her head as if to read him better, but he had no intention of saying more, lest he find himself trying to persuade her to accept. He'd never begged for a woman in his life and he wasn't about to begin.

'I...see.' She fiddled with the scarf knotted around her waist. So she was nervous after all. He told himself to back off, but he couldn't.

'And your answer?' The words were abrupt, not at all lover-like.

'I'll have to think about it.'

'*O seu Xeque é bastante atraente.*' Your sheikh is very handsome.

Even in Portuguese the words made Lina shiver. Not *her* sheikh, though she didn't bother to say that to Senhora Neves, sitting beside her at the royal feast.

But he could be yours. All you have to do is say yes.

A ripple of decadent delight shivered across Lina's skin, raising goosebumps against the slippery fabric of the dress she'd spent the afternoon finishing. She shifted in her seat, crossing her legs.

Would she say yes to his outrageous suggestion?

Could she?

It went against everything she'd been taught or ever expected for herself. Yet temptation was strong.

'*E ele olha para você o tempo todo.*' And he looks at you all the time.

Lina's head swung round towards the head of the table where Sayid was talking to one of his governors and Senhor Neves, the head of the Brazilian mining consortium bidding to open up newly discovered deposits of gems on the edge of the desert. The Emir's attention was fixed on his companions, not her.

If he'd glanced this way it was just to see if she was holding her own with Senhora Neves. The woman spoke no Arabic and little English and the interpreter Sayid had arranged had been struck down with tonsillitis.

Lina smiled. '*Ele está apenas preocupado com o meu Português.*' He's just worried about my Portuguese.

The other woman shook her head. '*Eu não acho que ele esteja a pensar em habilidades linguísticas.*' I don't think it's your language skills on his mind.

Heat scalded Lina's throat and cheeks. Surely he wasn't so obvious?

The older woman placed a hand on her arm and gently changed the subject, asking where Lina had purchased her dress, then expressing admiration when she discovered it was home-made.

Slowly Lina let herself relax. She should be pleased her rather basic Portuguese, learned from some of the girls at school, allowed her to keep Senhora Neves company tonight. Pleased too at the compliments over her dressmaking skill. She'd laboured over this dress, wanting to look her best so she wouldn't seem too out of place among tonight's sophisticated guests.

Who was she fooling? She wanted to look good for Sayid. Wanted him to admire her as he admired the women he usually invited to share his bed.

Why had he invited her to be his lover?

She still found it hard to believe he had. Tonight, as she entered the royal dining hall, he'd been cordial but aloof. There'd been nothing about his demeanour to hint he was interested in her personally apart from a momentary glint of speculation in those impenetrable eyes.

All she could think was that for some reason he wanted a change from his usual leggy blondes. She'd seen the photos of him accompanied by stunning socialites at events outside Halarq. Maybe he was bored and decided a brunette was as good a change as any.

Lina didn't fool herself that his emotions were involved. Except perhaps curiosity. She hadn't missed his surprise when she'd talked back to him this morning, demanding the freedom *not* to have a husband chosen for her.

That was it. She was a novelty.

She should be insulted, too proud to go to a man who made it clear all he wanted was short-term sex.

Except even short-term sex with Sayid was far too tempting. She'd tried to be interested in the men she'd met overseas, but none had lived up to the impossible standards Sayid had set with his sex appeal, understanding and shining generosity.

"4 for 4" MINI-SURVEY

We are prepared to **REWARD** you with 2 FREE books and 2 FREE gifts for completing our MINI SURVEY!

FREE
Value Over
$20!

You'll get...
TWO FREE BOOKS & TWO FREE GIFTS

just for participating in our Mini Survey!

Dear Reader,

IT'S A FACT: if you answer 4 quick questions, we'll send you 4 FREE REWARDS!

I'm not kidding you. As a leading publisher of women's fiction, we value your opinions… and your time. That's why we are prepared to **reward** you handsomely for completing our mini-survey. In fact, we have 4 Free Rewards for you, including 2 free books and 2 free gifts.

As you may have guessed, that's why our mini-survey is called **"4 for 4".** Answer 4 questions and get 4 Free Rewards. It's that simple!

Thank you for participating in our survey,

Pam Powers

To get your 4 FREE REWARDS:
Complete the survey below and return the insert today to receive 2 FREE BOOKS and 2 FREE GIFTS guaranteed!

"4 for 4" MINI-SURVEY

1 Is reading one of your favorite hobbies?
☐ YES ☐ NO

2 Do you prefer to read instead of watch TV?
☐ YES ☐ NO

3 Do you read newspapers and magazines?
☐ YES ☐ NO

4 Do you enjoy trying new book series with FREE BOOKS?
☐ YES ☐ NO

YES! I have completed the above Mini-Survey. Please send me my 4 FREE REWARDS (worth over $20 retail). I understand that I am under no obligation to buy anything, as explained on the back of this card.

❏ I prefer the regular-print edition
106/306 HDL GMYF

❏ I prefer the larger-print edition
176/376 HDL GMYF

FIRST NAME	LAST NAME

ADDRESS

APT.#	CITY

STATE/PROV.   ZIP/POSTAL CODE

READER SERVICE—Here's how it works:

Accepting your 2 free Harlequin Presents® books and 2 free gifts (gifts valued at approximately $10.00 retail) places you under no obligation to buy anything. You may keep the books and gifts and return the shipping statement marked "cancel." If you do not cancel, about a month later we'll send you 6 additional books and bill you just $4.55 each for the regular-print edition or $5.55 each for the larger-print edition in the U.S. or $5.49 each for the regular-print edition or $5.99 each for the larger-print edition in Canada. That is a savings of at least 11% off the cover price. It's quite a bargain! Shipping and handling is just 50¢ per book in the U.S. and 75¢ per book in Canada*. You may cancel at any time, but if you choose to continue, every month we'll send you 6 more books, which you may either purchase at the discount price plus shipping and handling or return to us and cancel your subscription. *Terms and prices subject to change without notice. Prices do not include applicable taxes. Sales tax applicable in N.Y. Canadian residents will be charged applicable taxes. Offer not valid in Quebec. Books received may not be as shown. All orders subject to approval. Credit or debit balances in a customer's account(s) may be offset by any other outstanding balance owed by or to the customer. Please allow 4 to 6 weeks for delivery. Offer available while quantities last.

► If offer card is missing write to: Reader Service, P.O. Box 1341, Buffalo, NY 14240-8531 or visit www.ReaderService.com ►

BUSINESS REPLY MAIL
FIRST-CLASS MAIL   PERMIT NO. 717   BUFFALO, NY

POSTAGE WILL BE PAID BY ADDRESSEE

READER SERVICE
PO BOX 1341
BUFFALO NY 14240-8571

NO POSTAGE
NECESSARY
IF MAILED
IN THE
UNITED STATES

She'd told herself her passion would fade but instead it had grown, becoming something profound and troubling that she couldn't shake off. It was more than the hero worship she'd experienced at seventeen. More than a first crush. If she wasn't careful, this could turn into an abiding passion and that would destroy her. Already she couldn't face the idea of being with any man other than Sayid. Which meant she needed, somehow, to cure herself of her feelings for him.

Surely she could do no better than follow his example. He kept his affairs short and never pined for a woman he'd set aside. He focused on lust and pleasure and wasn't bothered by troublesome yearnings for more.

Lina knew her yearnings were doomed. There could never be more with Sayid. It was become his temporary lover or nothing.

If she became his lover and eased this terrible yearning, surely the other feelings would fade? It had to be unrequited lust she felt, plus perhaps a shadow of her juvenile hero worship. Surely, after a week sharing his bed, she'd discover he had feet of clay. That he snored terribly or was a selfish lover or...

A trickle of heat slid down her spine. Slowly she turned her head towards the head of the table and found his heated, dark gaze on her. Her train of thought disintegrated and her breath jammed in her lungs as her blood took up a desperate tattoo of want.

She had to do *something* to end this. Sayid already had too much power over her. Now was the chance to make her own decision about her life.

The choice was simple. Retain her dignity and her

pride and work out her time doing community liaison until she was free to leave the palace and train as an interpreter. Or have a quick affair and walk away, hoping a week's intimacy would burn up this savage yearning for a man who could never be hers long-term.

Setting her jaw, she turned away from that glittering gaze and drew Senhora Neves into conversation.

She wasn't coming.

Disappointment lay heavy in his gut.

Sayid strode through his chambers, tearing off his headscarf and tugging at his fine robes. Despite the climate-controlled comfort of the royal feasting hall, he'd been burning up all night, on tenterhooks for some sign from Lina.

Never had he had to wait for a woman.

Never had a woman said she needed *time* to consider becoming his lover!

His teeth gritted as he hauled off his clothes and tossed them on a nearby chair. Even the scrape of fine cottons and silks against his flesh was like the rough graze of a blade. He was that aroused. And annoyed.

He hated teetering on the edge of restraint. He made his own decisions, shaping events the way he thought best. He did not do patience well, not when it meant handing power to another.

All evening he'd been aware of Lina, just a few seats down the dining table, wearing a sexy dress that covered her body yet clung to every curve. The purple had highlighted the colour of her eyes, and made the soft gold of her skin glow like fabled treasure.

His fingers had itched with the desperate urge to

reach for her, to stake his claim publicly in the face of so many admiring male glances.

But she hadn't given him the right.

Damn it! How had he gone from ruler of all he surveyed to a man desperate for a woman's nod of assent? As if he were a beggar awaiting her approval, not her lord and master.

A shudder racked his frame at the thought of the mastery he'd like to impose on her ripe, willing body.

Yet there was more than lust. There was admiration too, despite his frustration.

Sayid had watched her closely tonight, pride rising. She'd proved an able interpreter, despite her doubts since Portuguese wasn't her speciality. She'd also proved herself, again, adept at mixing with the wide range of people invited to these royal events.

Lina fitted in as if born to it, a real asset to the success of the evening. She was sociable and light-hearted yet ready to listen or keep the conversation flowing when necessary. She was good with people in a way he'd had to work at. Sayid had trained as a soldier and leader. Social chit-chat had taken time.

Rolling his shoulders against the stiffness there, he strode into the bathroom and wrenched on the shower. He didn't bother with the hot tap, simply let the needles of stinging cold massage his overheated flesh. He tried to blank his mind, or turn it to that new mining project and the problems of ensuring sustainability and long-term profitability.

It didn't work. Images of Lina swam before him. The decorous yet tantalising plunge of her V-necked dress that made him recall the soft press of her breasts when they'd kissed. Those sexy shoes that accentuated her long legs. Her animation. Her smiles as she spoke to Senhora Neves and her dinner companions and, in short, everyone but him.

With a growl he snapped off the water and stepped out, wrapping a towel around his waist and using another to wipe the water from his face.

Sleep was impossible. He might as well work instead. He stalked out of the bathroom and slammed to a halt.

He wasn't alone.

A figure stood poised in the open door from his bedroom into the courtyard.

A jolt of something like lightning struck, spearing Sayid, sending shockwaves from his scalp to the soles of his feet, scorching every centimetre between. For an instant the world stood absolutely, eerily still, before his heart hammered against his ribs like a runaway train and he swallowed hard, ignoring the razored obstruction in his suddenly dry throat.

'Lina.' His voice was gravel and hot tar, rumbling half an octave lower than its usual pitch.

Heat blasted his belly and after that moment's rampant acceleration his heartbeat slowed to a hard, ponderous, aching beat.

She stood on the threshold, neither in nor out of the room, hand braced on the window frame. Her face was composed but there was a tiny frown marring her smooth forehead and instinct screamed that she was torn between flight and entering.

Every cell of his body demanded that he prowl over there, wrap his arm around her and tug her inside. That he devour those delicious lips and then give free rein to the explosive, carnal hunger eating him up.

But Sayid retained just enough restraint to wait, even as his erection swelled needily. For he'd seen her eyes, bemused like a hunted animal facing a predator. He read doubt in her rigid form.

He had enough experience of women to know things would go far better if he let her believe it was her choice to stay with him. Never mind the fact that if she dared to try scurrying away now, he'd reach her in a few strides and seduce her into submission.

Breath tight in his lungs, he turned away and paced to the table where light refreshments were laid out for him. 'Come in. Please.'

He only released his breath when he heard the swish of her dress as she stepped inside.

Sayid took his time pouring a cold drink then turned to find her halfway across the room, her eyes veiled by long lashes as she looked down at the intricately woven tribal rug covering the middle of the floor.

'Here.' He approached slowly, pleased when she stood her ground. He passed the glass to her and she took it carefully, not letting her fingers touch his. She lifted it to her lips and swallowed as if parched from the desert sun.

'Thank you.' Her voice was husky but even. Then her eyes lifted to lock on his and another charge of electricity zapped him. That violet stare held wariness and…determination. It tracked down his bare torso then back to his face and Sayid felt it like a flame licking naked skin.

She held the glass out before her as if she'd forgotten it and Sayid took it from her, lifting it to his lips and downing the liquid in one swallow, easing his own arid throat.

Lina watched him swallow, her pupils dilating, and he heard the soft intake of her breath.

The air between them clogged in a haze of awareness, of heat and unmistakable desire. He defied her to deny it when every hitched breath, every tiny shudder in her taut frame proclaimed it.

'You came to give me your answer.' He turned to put the glass down, ostensibly giving her time to regroup, but actually seeking the strength to wait, not haul her to him and ravish her where they stood. Had he ever been so mightily aroused, just looking at a woman?

'I did. Yes.'

Sayid dragged air into his lungs, sliding the glass across the inlaid surface. 'Yes, you came to talk or yes, you agree to my proposal?'

'Yes, I—'

His eyes snapped to hers and again he heard that tiny catch of breath. The sound skittered over his bare flesh like a caress, drawing it impossibly tight.

This woman would be the death of him! They hadn't yet touched and he was bombarded with erotic sensations. He felt his patience shred, like ribbons snatched away in a *khamsin*, the unstoppable desert wind.

Her chin tipped higher. 'If you still want me, I'll be your lover for a week.'

Relief hummed through him.

If he still wanted her!

Couldn't she feel the charge between them?

Yet even as he wondered, he read the staunch pride

in the angle of her jaw and the blaze of her stunning eyes.

Of course she felt it. But this was a bargain—*his* bargain. Not some spur-of-the-moment impulse.

He owed her acknowledgement.

Gravely Sayid inclined his head, gesturing with his hand in the time-honoured way to signal respect and gratitude. For, despite his ravening impatience, he felt more than lust and relief. He…esteemed her.

None of his other lovers had stirred such respect, he realised. For them a fling with a rich man was easy and uncomplicated. He'd felt attraction and liking but no more.

Lina was different. Despite her western attitude to marriage and sex, her decision took guts. She wasn't from some faraway place where a short affair was condoned if not encouraged. The fact she'd taken all day to deliberate, when he knew she felt the same hunger he did, proved her choice wasn't made lightly.

'Thank you, Lina. I'm honoured by your decision.'

A shaky sigh escaped her. Instantly he wondered if his acknowledgement reinforced her qualms.

The idea of her having second thoughts was untenable.

Sayid crowded close, so close the purple folds of her skirt slid against his legs and his groin tightened needily. He'd kiss her into mindless pleasure—

Except, he realised as he bent his head, that would leave him mindless too. He stilled, recalling how last night's kiss had driven him to the edge.

He ached to taste her mouth again, lose himself in her welcoming sensuality. But if he kissed her on the lips the sex would be over in seconds and he wanted to savour their first time.

Abruptly Sayid straightened, noting with satisfaction her pouting lips and dazed, disappointed expression.

'Come.' Smiling, he took her small hand in his and led her towards the bed.

CHAPTER EIGHT

STRANGE HOW LINA'S quivers of nerves settled when Sayid took her hand and smiled, despite the hungry edge to his expression.

She *wanted* to be with him, wanted to learn with him the intimacies men and women shared, yet anxiety had undercut her decision. Anxiety that a week as his lover might cement rather than erode her feelings for him. Anxiety that he'd find her gauche or lacking with her total absence of sexual experience.

Even the heady moment when he'd acknowledged his respect for her had underscored the enormity of what she was doing.

But his smile, his touch, bathed her in a glow of delight and anticipation that obliterated all else.

This is right, her soul sang as they stopped by the bed.

So utterly right, her body crooned as they sank side by side onto the edge of the mattress.

Lina licked her lips, dry again despite the juice he'd shared with her, and saw with faint wonder the fixed way Sayid stared at her mouth. As if mesmerised. She registered the pulse suddenly noticeable at his temple. Tentatively she licked her bottom lip with the tip of her tongue again and felt a ripple pass through the big frame beside her.

But before complacency at her power could take hold he'd relinquished her hand, moving from the bed to the floor. Startled, she watched him kneel before her and lift her foot onto his thigh.

A quiver shot through her as those large, warm hands closed around her ankle, her nipples peaking in response to the darts of sensation spearing through her body. She had no name for them except possibly awareness, or need.

His smile was knowing but his shoulders were rigid with tension as he investigated the delicate suede ankle straps of her purple shoes.

'Sexy shoes,' he murmured as he tugged one tiny buckle undone and moved to the second.

'I...' She cleared her throat. 'I bought them the week before I came back to Halarq.' She didn't bother to add they were more daring and expensive than any shoes she'd ever owned. After years of frugal living, and with the shimmering purple fabric waiting to be made into a dress, Lina had succumbed to the urge for excitement and luxury. For who knew what life in Halarq would bring?

An affair with the Emir, that's what!

Even now she found it hard to believe. The sight of Sayid Badawi, kneeling before her, undoing her shoes as she'd once knelt before him, removing his boots, made her tremble.

Did he remember that night?

Even then, despite her fear, she'd been attracted to him. She'd decided it wouldn't be a hardship after all to share the Emir's bed. Yet that attraction was a mere shadow of her feelings for him now.

He removed her shoe and put it aside, then slowly, oh, so slowly, rubbed firm fingers the length of her sole and up her calf. Lina splayed her hands on the bed as her bones liquefied and pleasure swelled.

'Good?' She opened flickering eyelids to see his glittering gaze sweep over her.

'Marvellous.'

'But not as expert as you. You'll have to teach me.' He lifted her other foot onto his thigh and reached for the miniature buckles.

Lina said nothing, too swept away by his touch and the intoxicating notion that Sayid wanted to do this again, but even better, to please *her*.

A moan built at the back of her throat as he removed the second shoe and massaged his way from her foot, up her calf, to her knee and the sensitive spot behind it that she'd never known about.

When his mouth followed his hands in a torturously slow trail of open-mouthed kisses and licks, it was as if something snapped inside her. Her elbows gave way and she collapsed onto her back, waves of delight lapping higher and higher.

'Sayid.' It was a whispery breath, almost inaudible over the rush of blood in her ears.

Instantly the caresses paused. 'Yes?' She felt the word in a waft of warm breath against her knee. That caress, or perhaps the fact he'd stopped, seemingly attuned to her sudden tension, eased the nerves unexpectedly coiling in her belly.

'Just… Sayid.' For a moment she was overcome,

by the wonder of this man and what he did to her. Nothing had prepared her, and they'd only just begun.

Lina blinked and watched him rise over her, hands planted either side of her on the bed.

'You're safe with me, you know that, don't you?'

Of course she knew it. It was crazy to feel so emotional about what was, after all, the most natural thing in the world.

Besides, if her logic worked, a week of intimacy with Sayid would cure her of this emotional see-saw. She'd glut herself on him and be able to walk away, head up and heart whole. It *had* to work. The alternative was unthinkable.

'I know,' she whispered. 'I trust you.'

Which was all the encouragement he needed to slide her higher up the bed then lower himself beside her. In the move the towel at his hips came undone and Lina felt the hard, hot swell of his erection heavy on her thigh. She wrenched her gaze from his taut features, down that hard, muscled chest and lower, feeling nervous and fascinated at the same time. She wanted to trace the shape of him, discover how that hardness felt.

'Not a good idea.' Sayid's hand cuffed her wrist then brought it up to the mattress beside her ear.

'But I want to touch you.' Did she sound like a little girl deprived of a treat? There was nothing childish about how she felt.

He huffed out a laugh, yet the sound was stretched as if it covered pain. 'Later. Touch me now and this will be all over.'

Holding both her hands in his, he lowered his mouth, not to hers as she'd hoped, but to her neck, nipping with tiny bites that had her writhing till he swung a heavy thigh across her, pinioning her beneath him.

It was the most marvellous feeling, his weight pushing her down, evoking an instant need for her to rise against him, even though she had no desire to escape. But then Sayid pressed his lips to her décolletage, following the V neckline of her dress, and fire exploded in her veins. His lips, soft as a wisp of silk, brushed the upper slopes of her breasts again and again, and this time she couldn't stop the moan of pleasure.

'You're sensitive there.' His voice sounded hard, rough even, but there was definitely smugness in his eyes as he looked up at her. Then, holding her gaze he sank lower, drawing her nipple into his mouth and sucking hard through the fabric.

Lina jolted as if from an electric charge. Aftershocks radiated from her scalp right down to her toes.

'Shh, it's all right. I'll make it all right.' Sayid moved a little, hovered over her other breast then lowered his head again, this time gently scraping his teeth over her peaked nipple and making her cry out in wondrous delight.

Heaven help her. She was wound so tight she wouldn't survive much more of this.

'Please, Sayid.' She tried to reach for him but those strong hands still manacled her wrists as he teased her breasts with his mouth. 'It's not fair,' she gasped. 'You touch me but you won't let me touch you.'

He looked up, his mouth still closed around her nipple and the sight of him there sent a rush of liquid heat down to that needy place between her legs.

Finally he lifted his head. 'I never promised *fair*, Lina. But I promise you'll enjoy our time together.'

She had no trouble believing that. Already her body hovered near the brink of something momentous. The knowing gleam in his eyes told her Sayid understood exactly how to tip her off the edge.

'At least let me undress.' Because perversely, being fully clothed when he was naked felt almost embarrassing, because she was receiving all the pleasure and giving none. Or perhaps she was simply desperate to be one with him.

'Allow me.' He slid his hand under her shoulder and across to the zip at the back of her dress, lowering it so slowly Lina found herself arching her body against what felt like a caress.

When the zip was down, instead of peeling the dress from her shoulders, he grabbed the hem and lifted it by inching degrees up her legs. Lina found herself transfixed by the fierce intensity of his stare as he focused on revealing the bare skin of her legs. Finally there was a waft of air across her panties and she waited, breathless, for him to drag them down, or invite her to.

Instead, to her amazement, Sayid leaned down, nuzzling the flimsy damp fabric that hid her from his gaze.

Lina jumped as sensations she'd never known burst through her. She lifted her hands to push him away, then hesitated, fingers hovering above his head, mesmerised, as he kissed her again, right on that throbbing, swollen, exquisitely sensitive nub. Except it became more than a kiss as he drew hard, then kissed, then sucked hard again.

Suddenly light exploded in her soul, in her veins. Her vision blurred and she grabbed his head, hanging on for dear life as a cataclysm burst upon her, burning from the inside out, rolling through her in massive wave upon wave of delight.

Ecstasy.

As the universe-melding power of it eased and she came back to herself, Lina finally understood the meaning of the word. To stand outside yourself. She knew the dictionary definition, but never till this instant understood the stunning reality of it.

For moments there Lina had been both within her body and galaxies beyond it, exploding like a star in a distant solar system.

Slowly, infinitesimally slowly, her body floated back down to the bed, to limp satiation. To Sayid's tight smile and the high flags of colour across his cheeks. As if he'd got pleasure from her pleasure.

Except the proof that he was still unsatisfied lay heavy against her bare leg as he moved up beside her.

Abruptly embarrassment welled. Sayid had watched her come apart, more vulnerable than she'd ever been to anyone. It was another layer of self-possession peeled away by this man against whom she already had too few defences.

'I want to watch you come.' The words were out without her consciously forming them.

'That can be arranged.' His voice was gravel and black velvet. Yet he didn't move, instead meeting her stare with a look that told her he was trying to read her thoughts. 'You're not happy? What's wrong, Lina?'

Put like that, she felt ungrateful. What did she have to complain of when he'd given her such pleasure?

She'd heard enough gossip to know some men didn't feel obliged to satisfy their partner's needs. Far from being ungenerous, Sayid had taken her to the stars and back. And yet…

Lina reached out and cupped his face, feeling the tiny abrasions from what would become his beard. It was the first time she'd touched him like that and she revelled in her right to do so. Her hand splayed over the sharp angle of his jaw, fingers stroking his cheek. That was better, that connection.

'It was wonderful. Spectacular. But I don't want to be alone. I want you with me.'

She firmed her mouth, afraid of what her words would reveal. But instead of looking concerned, Sayid smiled and it was a caress, bathing her in luscious warmth.

'As I said, that can be arranged.'

After that Lina grew a little crazy, for Sayid stripped her of her clothes, but slowly, taking his sweet time peppering her with kisses and even, occasionally tiny nips that made her flesh tingle and need grow anew. He learned her body from the sensitive place behind her ears to her wrists where her pulse throbbed frantically. From the hollow near her hip bone, where his stubble was erotic bliss and torture at once, to her ankles which to her amazement were another erogenous zone when Sayid lavished attention there.

This time she got to touch too, to kiss and stroke him wherever she could reach. He tasted salty and rich, hot against her tongue. She loved the tiny little quivers under his skin when she found a particularly sensitive spot. Then he'd growl, low in his throat and whip his hand out, gently but firmly stopping her caresses as he took his time meandering over her body, turning it into an instrument tuned only to his touch.

She would have protested his determination to be in charge except she was too overcome by bliss.

Then, finally, she felt the feverish heat of his skin against hers, the hard-packed weight of him brushing her from breasts to thighs.

Propped on one elbow he peered down at her while his other hand stroked the damp curls between her legs and she juddered against his touch.

This time when she slid her hand downwards he didn't stop her and she encountered the hot, rigid swell of his arousal. He'd put on a condom she realised as her fingers closed around him. She hadn't even been aware of him doing that. But what occupied her thoughts was the nervous certainty that there was no way this could work. She was an average-sized woman but Sayid was—

'Lift your knees, Lina.' Already he was palming her inner thigh, lifting it up against the jut of his hip. Instinctively she bent her other knee, cradling him between her thighs.

'Sayid…' She wanted this but it struck her that perhaps this wouldn't be as simple as she'd imagined. 'We need to talk.'

His mouth covered hers, blocking her words. At the same time she felt him move between her legs. 'Later, sweet Lina. I can't wait any longer.' He pulled her hand away from him, then slid his hand under her, tilting her pelvis higher as with one smooth movement he thrust.

Her gasp was eaten up by his ravenous mouth, tongue probing and caressing in a way that sent her senses reeling. Just as the feel of him pushing deep sent waves of shock pulsing through her.

Lina felt pressure, so much pressure. But the insistent drag of his mouth against hers and his harsh hum of approval counteracted her sudden tension.

He stilled. She felt the rise and fall of his heavy chest against hers. In that instant she registered the unfamiliar tickle of the hair on his thighs, the rigidity of his muscled arms where she grabbed him and a scent, musky and rich, unfamiliar yet enticing.

He began to withdraw and immediately Lina wrapped one leg high over his hip, trying to hold him close. This wasn't…comfortable, but she wanted it all.

Sayid's head lifted, ebony eyes snaring hers. She heard the sound of rasping breaths in the still night air.

'I'm hurting you.' She wouldn't have recognised it as his voice, so rough and thick.

'You're not.' There was discomfort and a strangeness, but no pain. 'Besides, you promised.'

'Promised?' He spoke through clenched teeth and for the first time Lina noticed the sheen of sweat glazing his bronzed features. Belatedly she realised the powerful muscles in his arms were quivering with tension, the pulse at his temple hammering.

She did that to him. She stroked her hands up to his shoulders and felt him shudder. For reasons she didn't fully understand, the realisation of his vulnerability made her body soften against him.

'That I could watch you come.'

His eyes blazed down at her but Lina didn't fear him now. She slipped her hands up to anchor at the back of his neck and lifted her other leg, locking her ankles across his back, holding herself to him as surely as he held her.

Immediately he slipped further into her cradling body, so when the slide became a thrust Lina's moment of smugness evaporated in a gasp of astonishment. It felt as if Sayid was planted so deep within that he touched her heart.

Then there was no time for thought as he withdrew, only to arch his spine and push back again, then again. Each surge seated him further and each movement caused a delicious friction that created delight and a hunger for more. She lifted herself against each thrust, addicted to the feelings he evoked.

Dark eyes held hers as his tempo increased and with it her body's sensitivity. Lina tightened the clasp of her legs, just as Sayid slipped his hand between their bodies and lightly touched her clitoris. A second later he powered hard against her and the world burst into flame.

There was a cry of wonder, a moment of strained disbelief, then rapture engulfed her just as Sayid arched his neck and pumped hard into her, spilling himself in a throb of ecstasy.

Through the whirl of sensation, the blurred, overwrought senses and piercing delight, Lina watched him lose himself in her. It was as if he fought a great battle but finally, as rapture took them both, his head fell to her neck, his breath searing her flesh, and they were one.

A great well of protectiveness filled Lina. She wrapped her arms around him, adoring the weight of his slumped body, the intimacy of their joined bodies and the intensity of the connection. Even now echoes of pleasure rippled through her, set off by Sayid's occasional shudders. Her body fed off his and vice versa.

She'd never felt closer to another person in her life.

Then, with a mighty groan, Sayid rolled away to lie on his back beside her. His eyes were closed and he said nothing and Lina didn't have the strength to object, though she'd much rather he'd stayed where he was.

Finally, her catapulting heart began to slow and her body floated in a dreamy state between bliss and sleep, despite the unfamiliar throb between her legs.

She had no idea how long they lay like that. She didn't have words to describe what they'd shared, and didn't want to think about what she ought to say, if anything.

Finally, through a drifting haze, Lina felt Sayid move. Slitting her eyes open she saw him get up and walk towards the bathroom. The subtle lamplight played on the powerful lines of his tall frame, the clench and release of his rounded buttocks. Even after that cataclysmic orgasm he walked like a prince, head up, shoulders back, with the easy grace of an athlete.

Not as if his world had reeled off its axis and gone spinning out of orbit.

He took sex in his stride, of course. He was an experienced lover, no doubt used to the overwhelming tide of bliss that left her weak and trembling. Plus, everyone said sex was different for men—they were adept at not getting emotionally involved.

Slowly, every movement a triumph of will over a body too lethargic to respond easily to her brain's commands, Lina rolled onto her side, tucking her feet up and her hands beneath her chin.

Bliss still echoed through her body and befuddled her thoughts. Yet one fact shone clear and ineluctable. She'd been afraid that sex with Sayid would be playing with fire, that it might inflame rather than obliterate her feelings for him. She'd been right. She wasn't merely playing with fire. She'd stepped right into the inferno and she feared there was no way out.

Lina let her heavy eyelids close, too exhausted even to panic yet. It was enough to lie here, boneless and sated beyond her imaginings, breathing in the scent of sex and Sayid, feeling the strange, heavy emptiness between her legs where he'd been.

Wetness spilled over her cheeks and across her nose. Not tears of distress or worry, but of wonder at the sheer beauty of what they'd shared. She'd wipe them away when she found the energy to lift her arm again.

For now all she could do was wonder how she was going to sever her feelings for Sayid when tonight had only drawn her closer to him. She feared she was falling in love with him.

CHAPTER NINE

SAYID LOOKED DOWN at the sleeping woman curled up at the very edge of his broad bed. Her pose was that of a child seeking comfort with her limbs tucked tight against her.

But there was nothing childlike about her body. Even now, still stunned by the roaring intensity of that powerful orgasm, his gaze roved over her hungrily. He wanted to slide his hand over those hypnotically perfect curves, taste the dark raspberry nipple that peeked at the edge of her folded arm, tangle himself in the precious silk of her hair and lose himself all over again.

No, there was nothing childlike about Lina's body. Or about the way she'd wanted him. Another unseen jab to his body, this time lower, as he recalled her declaring she wanted to watch him come. A great shudder tore through him. Sayid had almost lost it when she said that. Only the determination to take her over the edge with him had seen him through.

Nor had there been anything innocent about the way she'd wrapped herself around him, clinging as if to stop him withdrawing. As if! Nothing on this earth could have prevented him enjoying their union to the full. Even the realisation she was, against all expectation, a virgin.

A deep breath stretched him but didn't alleviate the strange tightness banding his ribs. He flexed his hands then clasped them behind his back, away from the temptation to reach out and touch her.

Why hadn't she told him?

He supposed that was what she'd been going to say until he'd stopped her words, too impatient to listen.

But how could she be so innocent? She was twenty-two. She'd been living in the west for years and he had no doubt western males were no more immune to her beauty and charm than he. In fact he had proof. Look at the way that American had hung on her every word the other night. For that matter, she'd been a magnet for male attention since her teens.

While overseas, Lina had been free of the strict chaperonage usual in Halarq. Why hadn't she taken advantage of her freedom?

Innocent she might have been, but there was no mistaking her for anything other than an incredibly sensual woman, with a profound capacity for pleasure. The fact she hadn't given in to the natural urges of her body before intrigued him.

Sayid stifled the heavy tension brewing in his lower body. Clearly he was not going to wake her for more sex, no matter that he was, if possible, even more desperate for her than he'd been an hour ago. She'd been exquisitely responsive but her body's tightness told its own story. She'd be sore now.

Yet he moved closer, drawn by a mix of emotions he refused to catalogue. He told himself a simple sense of responsibility topped the list. He'd seduced an innocent—a first for him as he'd scrupulously pursued only experienced women till Lina. He was obliged to care for her.

Obligation. Was that what he felt?

She shifted and his belly clenched. Were those dried tears on her cheeks?

He stood transfixed, struggling to cope with unaccustomed guilt.

She moved again and he told himself it had been a trick of the light. She was exhausted, that was all, and who could blame her? Even he had been stunned by what they'd shared.

Yet a baffling tide of emotion rose, confounding him. He needed to do something, fix things. Except nothing could undo what he'd done.

And, the savage inside him acknowledged, he didn't want to. A more civilised man would regret stealing her virginity. Sayid couldn't.

Hell, no decent man would proposition her the way he had!

Yet Sayid wouldn't change a thing. How could he when his craving for Lina was unchanged? In fact it was stronger than before. At least before tonight he hadn't savoured her fiery passion, hadn't watched her come apart for him, or drowned his senses in her welcoming body.

Enough!

He was hard with a carnal hunger that had barely eased, despite the long, cold shower he'd endured. But he wouldn't act…not yet.

Nor could he let her go. He knew his limits and he was far too selfish for that. But he could at least respect her need to rest.

Sayid bent and picked up the sheet, pulling it up over Lina's shoulder, covering her nakedness.

Lina didn't know what woke her. She was cocooned in the most scrumptiously comfortable bed, content as a cat in the sun. She'd never felt so good.

Lazily she stretched and instantly registered two things. The hint of heaviness inside, up between her thighs, and the fact she wasn't curled up on a sheet but on a body.

Her eyes snapped open. In the faint grey pre-dawn light she saw her pillow was a male chest, powerful and with a light covering of black hair. A second later she realised the steady pulse in her ears wasn't hers, but came from that same chest, where she rested her head.

'Good morning.' The sound rumbled up from beneath her.

Lina had thought nothing could match the intimacy of making love with Sayid, but waking with him, *feeling* the throb of his heart and the ripple of his baritone voice, made her experience again the connection that had dazzled her last night.

To her consternation, nerves hit. It was one thing allowing him to sweep her into a firestorm of longing where, in her greed for him, she abandoned any trace of modesty. It was another to face him the morning after.

Hands splayed on his warm chest, she lifted her head.

Even in this dim light he was stunning, his charisma due as much to that aura of strength as the slightly stern yet wholly handsome features. His jaw was dark with the hint of a beard and his eyes mesmerising.

Lina felt them bore right into her, probing her secrets, stripping away whatever layers of protection she retained against him. Her breath caught. Sayid was beautiful in the pared back, almost harsh way of the desert, sculpted by wind and sun yet with a magnificence that stole the breath.

'Good morning,' she croaked. It was hard to believe last night wasn't a fantasy, despite waking against him.

Then, abruptly, his mouth widened into a smile and something contracted deep inside her chest. Last night he'd been serious, his smile tight. Sometimes he'd even looked as if he was in pain. This…this was glorious.

Sayid lifted his head and crushed her lips with his. Instantly Lina opened her mouth, leaning in for more, but he was already pulling back.

'How are you this morning, Lina?' Despite the approval in those gleaming eyes, his tone was serious.

'Fine. And you?'

He shook his head. 'How are you really? I wasn't as…gentle as I might have been. Are you hurting?'

Something within her, some shred of the cloistered girl she'd once been, shrivelled in embarrassment. But Lina reminded herself she was a new woman. A woman who made her own decisions. Who reached out for what she wanted. Who wasn't ashamed of her feelings, or the bargain she'd made with Sayid. Who'd positively revelled in what they'd done last night.

'No.' Then, when his eyes narrowed, 'Not really *sore*.' It was more an awareness of part of her body she'd never felt before. But that was too much detail.

'You should have told me.' His expression turned grave, his smile fading. '*Before* we went to bed.'

Lina levered herself higher, putting distance between them, till one hot, sinewy arm wrapped around her waist, anchoring her to him. Nerves jumped beneath her skin and suddenly that awareness of her body became a throb of emptiness.

Did it really take so little to make her ready for Sayid? Not just ready but eager?

Of course she'd need more than one measly night to satisfy her greed for him. It was nothing to worry about, despite last night's fears she was in over her head.

'Why? Would you have stopped? Would you have withdrawn your proposition?'

His nostrils flared as he breathed hard, his chest pushing up against her. Lina was aware of him all down her body, including, she realised, the solid ridge of his erection against her inner thigh. Restlessly she shifted, discovering a fine layer of cotton separating their lower bodies. Strange how familiar and enticing, yet how shockingly…dangerous they felt together.

Sayid's other hand clamped her bare buttocks, holding her still, which was when she realised he wore loose trousers. Why? Because he didn't want more sex? But that erection surely proved—

'Stop twitching!' His voice was terse, almost hoarse.

Lina blinked, absorbing the tension in his starkly beautiful features. A tension that hadn't been there earlier.

Because she'd rubbed against him? The possibility she wielded such power was exciting yet a tiny bit scary. This was all so new. New and, she decided as she tilted her hips just a fraction, delicious.

'Lina!' His voice was pure growl this time. She was still absorbing the feral sound when he surged up, flipping her over onto her back and weighing her down with his tall frame, his thighs bracketing hers as if to stop her escaping.

Lina had no wish to escape. Every part of her body stirred and snapped with energy. Her blood fizzed and everywhere they touched she felt tingles of—

His mouth covered hers and instantly she was lost. His mouth, the slow, deliberate, possessive slide of his tongue against hers, was the epicentre of her world. His kiss drew her back into that swirling, sensual realm of pleasure she'd discovered last night.

Lina's hands moulded his hard chest then insinuated themselves up, over his shoulders, to anchor in his hair, pressing him close.

When he pulled his head up from the kiss they were both breathing heavily. Reluctantly she opened her eyes.

Sayid's mouth was a thin line, taut as if with displeasure.

'What is it?' Lina wanted to smooth away the furrow at the centre of his forehead almost as much as she wanted him to kiss her again.

Because it's not just sex you want, is it? You care for him.

The truth ripped through her languid feeling of well-being.

As if he needs you to care or look after him.

The idea of Sayid, capable, clever and in command

of a whole nation, needing anyone, much less someone like her to care for him was patently absurd.

That didn't stop her lifting her head and planting a kiss on his jaw, then another, till he reared even further back, creating distance between them. Her head fell back onto the pillow, a discomfiting twist tightening her chest.

He disapproved of her kissing him uninvited?

Sayid shook his head as if clearing his thoughts. When he spoke his voice was harsh. 'You asked if I'd have stopped last night if I knew you were a virgin.' He hefted a breath that expanded his chest mightily. 'It would be nice to say yes, I'd have stopped, but it's not true.' His gaze bored into her. 'I've always tried to be an honourable man and deflowering virgins is something I've avoided. But with you…' Again that quick shake of his head as if exasperated. 'From the moment you appeared in the doorway last night you were destined for my bed, Lina. Nothing would have held me back.'

He didn't look happy about it. In fact he looked positively grim. Whereas Lina glowed, hearing his words. It had been the same for her. She'd tried so long to argue herself out of wanting Sayid but nothing, neither logic nor pride had stopped her.

'I'm glad,' she whispered, lifting her hand to his jaw, fascinated by the way his eyelids flickered as she caressed the roughened skin there. 'I didn't want you to hold back. I want you to want me.'

Sayid's bark of laughter was short and sharp. Even the gentle touch of her soft fingers across his chin weakened his resolve to take things slow and gentle this morning out of consideration for her untried body.

'Oh, I want you all right, Lina. The problem is restraining myself.'

That luxurious mouth pouted, making his gut contract and his need spike. 'I don't want you restrained.' He felt the hitch of her soft breasts teasing his chest, and realised he'd forgotten to keep his distance and had sunk down again, lying over her skin to skin. 'I just want you.'

Her words painted a picture he tried to dismiss and couldn't. Of giving himself up utterly to his need for her.

'I'm glad you're so eager after your first time.' He'd feared she'd be wary this morning, possibly regretting her decision to come to him, or at least feeling sore and disinclined for sex. Still, she didn't understand what she was saying. She had no idea what a demanding lover he could be.

Sleeping beside her all night, or more accurately lying awake fighting the urge to have her again, had been one of the most difficult things Sayid had done.

'But why wait till now to lose your virginity?' That had troubled him through the long, frustrating night. 'I assumed you'd had lovers before, especially since you're not interested in marriage. Yet you saved yourself, as if for marriage.'

Lina's gaze slid from his, her eyelids dropping to veil her bright eyes. Instantly Sayid was alert. He'd touched a nerve and, judging by her reaction, she didn't want to discuss it.

'It's no big deal, is it? Everyone has a first time.'

Sayid put his weight on one arm and with his other

hand tipped her chin up till she couldn't escape his scrutiny.

'What are you hiding, Lina?'

Her eyes opened wide. He wanted to read her thoughts, her secrets, but he found himself drowning in that brilliant purple-blue gaze.

'I'm not hiding anything.' Yet he caught the thread of agitation in her voice and in her quickening heartbeat, hammering against him.

She must have read his scepticism for she snatched a quick breath. Sayid had to fight to ignore how her nipples scraped against him as her breasts lifted.

'Look, I grew up in a traditional house, okay? My mother might have been a dancer once, and her reputation suffered with the old biddies in the town as a result, but if anything that made her even more determined to protect mine. The only men I saw growing up were relatives and close friends of the family, usually my father's age. I had no chance or inclination to go to bed with a man. Especially when I saw the way some of them looked at my mother, despite the fact she was married.'

Sayid experienced a ripple of distaste. He guessed the young Lina hadn't had a good opinion of the men she'd met. And then there were her cousins, trying to take advantage of her in her own home.

'I was brought up to think the only man I'd sleep with would be my husband.'

'Until your uncle sent you here.' A sliver of guilt needled Sayid. He hadn't taken advantage of her then, but now—

'And you gave me an opportunity I could never have imagined.' Her smile broke his train of thought.

'For the first time you gave me power over my own life. You gave me my freedom, and the right to choose.'

'But you didn't exercise that choice while you were overseas. Why not?' Increasingly he found it hard to concentrate. Partly because of that sunshine of a smile beaming up at him and partly because lying body to body was too arousing. He wanted to get to the bottom of Lina's decision but his need to know was becoming obscured by the need for sex.

Her expression sobered, even as she lifted her hand to smooth her palm over the upper slope of his chest. Tingles of want spread through his body.

'Why should I? It's not something to rush into. Does it really matter since in the end I chose you?'

Sayid struggled to think, to process the meaning behind Lina's words. On the face of it, no, it didn't matter. He should be pleased she'd taken up his scandalous proposition and gave herself to him.

Yet there was something…cagey about her. He sensed an unwillingness to talk on this. A disinclination to discuss something so personal? Or maybe someone had broken her heart while she was away? If he discovered someone had hurt her…

Anger throbbed through him at the idea, but before it could take hold Lina linked her fingers around his neck and tugged, inviting his kiss.

For a moment Sayid withstood the invitation. His gut warned she was holding something back and it bothered him that he had no idea what it was. He didn't like mysteries, especially as he sensed this could be important.

'Sayid? Don't you want to kiss me?' Her expression grew tentative and he heard the tiniest hint of a tremor in her voice. It was a reminder of her almost total lack of experience.

'How can you doubt it?' He moved, angling his body so his erection aligned perfectly between her legs.

Her eyelids fluttered as he tilted his hips, pressing so that, if he hadn't put on loose trousers, he'd be entering her. His pulse jumped at the thought.

Seconds later he was skimming the trousers down his legs and kicking them off, reaching across to the bedside table for protection.

Postponing the discussion was a deliberate decision, he assured himself as he rolled on the condom. Lina's reticence was natural modesty, that was all. He didn't need to understand everything about her to enjoy sex with her.

In the past it had suited him perfectly not to delve too deep into the thoughts and motivations of his lovers. It was all part of keeping a suitable detachment.

Ruthlessly Sayid muted the voice protesting that he *wanted* to understand everything about Lina. Proclaiming too that his urgency now was proof that his vaunted self-restraint had cracked, if not shattered.

Sayid stilled, trying to summon that restraint.

Then Lina put her hand on his chest, right above his thudding heart. Her fingers slid slowly down, over ribs that tightened at her touch, skimming his belly that twitched and trembled at the caress. Lower.

Explosions detonated through his body as her small hand closed tentatively around him. Sayid's breath stalled as her fist glided down his length then paused. The arm propping him up on the bed shook like a Bedouin tent in a sandstorm.

'Harder.' The word was gruff, almost indecipherable. Yet Lina understood. Her grip firmed as it slid, centimetre by torturously slow centimetre, back to the tip.

Sayid shut his eyes as they rolled back in his head. Her caress wasn't practised or smooth but he'd never felt such raw delight at a woman's touch.

Why? The word drummed an incessant staccato beat in his head.

But it was drowned by the rush of blood evacuating his brain and heading lower. He'd been stiff as a board but now he grew in her hand, pressing into that warm caress that slid down his shaft then up, more confident and devastating with each pass.

Dimly Sayid recalled the need for control, but it was swept away as he bucked into Lina's hold, unable to stop himself.

He snapped his eyes open, falling into her violet gaze. The rich scent of roses and female arousal filled the air.

She squeezed him and he jolted. Any second now…

Gritting his teeth, Sayid plucked her hand away, shuddering at the slide of her fingers against his erection.

He saw a protest form on those plump lips but he wasn't in the mood for conversation. His mouth crashed down on hers in a kiss that was barely short of brutal, devouring her with a hunger he was past restraining.

Sayid covered her mound with his hand, relishing the way she tilted up into his touch. That was it. He just needed to check… Yes. Triumph stirred. Lina was ready for him.

He'd learned how to make foreplay an art, priding

himself on his patience, ensuring his lover's satisfaction first. But now there was no time for subtlety or patience. He braced himself over her and with one purposeful thrust, pushed hard, harder, only to find himself sliding with incredible ease right to her core.

Stunned eyes, the colour of mountain irises, met his. For an instant the world held steady. Then, before he had time to expend the breath cramming his lungs, or even think about technique, the pressure hit like a runaway train, smashing into him.

Lina clenched around him again and again, a flush tinting her bare breasts, throat and cheeks, a look of astonishment on her face.

Then Sayid was incapable of noticing anything but the unholy tightness in his groin, the rush of volcanic pleasure pulsing through him, and the tug of muscles stretched to breaking point as instinct took over and he pumped frantically into oblivion.

Dimly he heard a guttural cry of triumph and a sob of what he hoped was feminine delight, as his strength gave way and he crashed down on Lina.

He had to move away. He had to get off her. But the strength had seeped from his body. Besides, there was a warm, rhythmic stroke over his back that urged him not to move. His head was in the curve of Lina's shoulder, his chest crushing her.

Finally, gathering his wits, he lifted his weight onto his elbows. Instantly she murmured a protest, her arms wrapping around his back, pulling as if to tug him down. Sayid pressed a kiss to the slick, perfumed skin of her neck, then forced himself to roll away, onto his side. The slide of their exquisitely sensitive bodies separating made him shudder.

At last he lay on his back, trembling. Undone.

He'd thought last night a pinnacle of physical pleasure.

This was…miraculous. Appallingly, outrageously, infinitely better than he'd experienced before.

His befuddled brain tried to compute a reason for it. His longish stint of celibacy. Muddled perception after a sleepless night. Some secret thrill at bedding a virgin.

No. Nothing accounted for it.

Sayid huffed a laugh. Maybe, after years of practice, he'd just got it right for the first time. The way he felt, anything was possible.

'What's so funny?'

'Me. My brain's short-circuited.' Eyes still closed, he reached out and groped for her hand. 'Are you okay?'

'I'm not sure.' Lina hesitated and despite believing he'd never move again, Sayid found himself propped on one arm, looking down at her. Lina's hair was spread behind her like a dark halo, her raspberry-tipped breasts trembled with each shaky breath she took and her skin was flushed.

'Did I hurt you?' His belly crawled at the idea.

Instantly that vibrant gaze meshed with his. Another tiny tremor, like an echo of rapture, wove through him.

'Of course not. It was…' She shook her head. 'I don't have words. But you didn't hurt me. I just never knew anything could feel so good. I feel…changed.' She chewed on her lip. 'Is it always like this?'

Relief made him smile. 'Rarely. Obviously we're very attuned to each other.'

'Oh. That explains it.' She rolled onto her side, moving close. 'Will you hold me please? I feel… I don't want to be alone.'

Sayid stared down at the woman burrowing into his chest and told himself he didn't do cuddles. Post-coital snuggling was to be avoided in case a lover began to get sentimental. It had been a problem in the past occasionally, despite his precautions.

But instead of moving away, Sayid slipped his left arm under her head, pulling her across so she was draped over him. His right arm wrapped automatically around her, drawing her snug against him.

'Nice,' she murmured in a blurred voice and despite himself Sayid grinned.

But as Lina fell into an untroubled sleep and the rising sun sent shafts of pink and apricot across the room, his smile died.

He'd lost control, spectacularly. And, if he was honest with himself, he'd do it again in an instant if there was a chance of experiencing something like that exaltation as he lost himself in Lina.

Lina. That was what was different.

He'd told himself sex with Lina was like sex with any other woman, but it wasn't true.

She had some effect on him he didn't understand. She'd decimated his command of himself. No, *obliterated* it.

Gut instinct warned of trouble. What sort he couldn't fathom. But there was something about Lina that threatened more than his tight rein over his sensual nature.

He could walk away from this deal, tell her one night had been enough and a week wasn't necessary.

Except, he realised as his hold on her tightened and his soul howled silently in protest, he didn't want to. For the first time in his adult life Sayid found himself unable to master his desire.

He wanted her and he intended to keep her.

For a week. That was all.

What disruption could a single week cause?

CHAPTER TEN

DAY FIVE AND there was no lessening of his hunger for Lina.

Had he really expected there would be?

To be fair, he hadn't had her solely to himself. Usually when he took a lover he was with them around the clock, often at some discreet luxury resort where he could sate his senses without distraction. On those vacations he'd manage the most urgent matters via email and phone for a few hours a day, since the business of ruling could never be avoided completely.

Now, however, he hadn't had an opportunity to re-organise his schedule to accommodate a break. Sayid struggled to cram his normal workload and his time with Lina into too-short days. It drove him crazy, for he couldn't get enough of her. He'd sit in meetings, distracted by the memory of her and the sex they'd had, or planning the sex they'd have when his interminable day of appointments was over.

He should have planned this better, so he could take her somewhere and devote himself to the passion searing just as white-hot now as it had been in the beginning. Each day it became more apparent that seven nights with her in his bed wouldn't be enough.

The idea scraped like a rusty spike through his belly. He'd never needed more than a week with any woman, no matter how charming or beautiful.

For Lina's sake, he maintained the illusion they weren't lovers. He refused to risk her reputation even more by clearing his diary and whisking her off to a secluded love nest. Publicly they were ward and guardian. Sayid was conscious of the need to protect her from gossip that would make things difficult for her when they separated. He could only hope loyalty from the staff who knew her suite adjoined his would prevent gossip.

Yet each day Sayid found himself altering his schedule to see her. Yesterday he'd suggested to Senhor Neves that his wife might like to join them on a site visit so she could see the countryside. As she and Lina had become friends, and the Portuguese interpreter was only slowly recovering from illness, Lina came too.

Sayid's attention had strayed time and again. He spent far too much time noticing the way Lina got on, not just with the foreigners, but the locals who'd come to hear about the mine project.

There'd been concerns about environmental issues, which was why Sayid himself had attended. But the meat of the concerns hadn't been raised straight away. Initially discussions were stilted and formal, to be expected between a ruler and his people, yet frustrating when Sayid wanted to hear the truth. Specific fears had only been raised after he'd lingered over mint tea with the local sheikh and his extended family, and the womenfolk had broken the ice, establishing a surprising level of rapport that eased the whole discussion.

Sayid understood his Minister for Education's comments about Lina's charm being worth a dozen professional consultants. For years Sayid had sought to establish a better relationship with his people and he'd made some progress, but being supreme ruler created an automatic distance. With Lina bridging that gap it was much easier. He'd learned more about local concerns in that one morning visit than he had in six official reports.

Now, today Sayid cancelled a late meeting in order to accept an invitation he'd usually politely decline. A wedding feast celebrated by the community he'd visited last week, when he'd seen the bride-to-be and Lina practising a bridal dance.

'They will be thrilled at your attendance,' his secretary, Makram, said as he frowned down at his diary. 'It will be an unexpected honour.' Valiantly he sought to suppress his curiosity.

Much as he valued Makram, Sayid had no intention of explaining his decision to attend. This time it had nothing to do with being more accessible to his people and everything to do with Lina. She'd be at the wedding which would run into the evening.

Sayid had bitten back a protest at the news. When his official duties were done each day he wanted her with *him*.

Surely she was as eager as he to be alone together?

As if reading his carefully camouflaged discontent she'd admitted she'd prefer to return early, but she'd given her word to be there for the dancing.

Sayid was torn between annoyance and admiration at her determination to keep her word.

Which was how he found himself, as the sun set,

guest of honour at festivities on the edge of the desert. City dwellers though they were, these families kept the Halarqi custom of marking major events outdoors.

It had been a long time since Sayid attended such a celebration. That explained his interest in the dancers. Yet it was hard not to stare at the one wearing an indigo dress with crimson and silver ornamentation.

Every dip and sway of Lina's body reminded him of how she responded to the thrust of his own when he took her. The spiralling, delicate movements of her fluttering hands and slim arms recalled the feel of her fingers raking his scalp, as she hugged him tight. The supple, whirling movements, almost balletic in their precision, made him recall in heated detail her passionate physicality.

Lina was no shrinking violet in bed. She was exuberant and responsive. She never denied him and was gratifyingly enthusiastic as he expanded her sexual experience.

They were an excellent match.

Heat speared his lower body as her eyes caught his. The silver collar around her throat shifted as she turned and Sayid caught a hint of redness at the base of her neck.

Stubble rash. He'd forgotten to shave last night and this morning she'd borne evidence of his caresses across her neck, breasts and lower.

Seeing the marks of his passion stirred guilt.

And a disquieting possessiveness.

As if he wanted to brand her publicly, announcing his ownership so no other man would dare look at her the way they did now—avid and enthusiastic.

Sayid hated the unfamiliar sense of powerlessness

he experienced, unable to claim her as his, to stop others salivating over her. He could proclaim her his mistress but for her sake he didn't.

'Your Highness?' He turned to find his host bowing low. 'Would it please you to see the archery?'

Sayid wanted to stay here, watching Lina. Which was why he instantly got to his feet. He was not and never had been the sort of man to sigh over a woman.

'I'd be delighted. And are those preparations for a riding display too?'

He turned away from the dancing, ignoring an internal pang of protest. He refused to behave like a smitten teenager who had eyes for no one but his girl. Yet walking away was far harder than anything else he'd done all day.

'Isn't he spectacular?' The girl next to her sighed. 'I wish my parents could find me a man like that to marry.'

Lina's chest tightened, squeezing her lungs, or was it her heart? It had to be from the exertion of the dance. It was nothing to do with the idea of Sayid as a bridegroom, about to marry some eager young woman.

For it was Sayid they watched.

They'd seen the end of the archery contest, drawn by the gasps and applause of the crowd. To Lina's surprise Sayid had wielded a powerful bow as easily as she did a needle and thread. To the crowd's delight, and hers, he'd only been beaten by a single shot in the last round. The winner turned out to be the state champion but it was their Emir who the crowd applauded.

Now, rather than retiring to the seat provided for

him, Sayid joined some of the other men in a display of horsemanship.

Of course he rode. He had the heavily muscled thighs of a horseman and the strong, clever hands.

Though to say he rode didn't do him justice. Lina's gaze was riveted as he completed a circuit of the field. Deftly he wove through obstacles as easily as if he and the horse were one, then used a traditional horseman's lance to capture a flaming hoop two others had failed to snatch.

Around them the crowd roared and the girl beside her sighed and clapped.

'Oh, isn't he wonderful? Wouldn't you like a man just like that?'

Lina's instant agreement died in her throat, pain settling like a boulder, crushing her insides. For she wanted it too much. Not just any man, and not simply because he was athletic and impressive, but because he was Sayid.

She wanted him. Badly.

For five days she'd been his secret lover and the desire for him had grown, not lessened.

But it wasn't just desire, was it?

Lina wanted more, so much more. The idea of him performing these feats one day at his wedding celebration to some sophisticated woman of his own class made her nauseous. She grimaced, tasting the ashes of stupid, impossible dreams on her tongue.

Stoically she told herself that whatever the future held, she'd wish Sayid well—a happy marriage to a loving wife and the blessing of children.

The thought stirred a savage jab of pain right through her ribs and she stiffened, breathing through the ache.

'He's certainly memorable,' she murmured eventually.

'And to think you see him all the time. How lucky you are.'

Silently Lina nodded, her eyes still on Sayid. Lucky didn't begin to describe it. What were the chances a man like Sayid would ever be interested in someone like her? Their week together was an amazing, glorious experience and she intended to hoard the memory of it close through the long, lonely time ahead.

Now he drew the horse up amongst the other riders, a grin splitting his proud features as they chatted. This was another side to Sayid and he fascinated her. Not the passionate, generous lover who gave her delight beyond anything she'd imagined. Not the serious, guarded ruler with the weight of a nation on his shoulders, but a man of vibrant energy and good humour. A man other men respected as one of their own, not simply because he was their Emir.

Lina swallowed hard. Sayid was charismatic in a way that had little to do with his royal position. It was no wonder she was…a little blinded by him. Her feelings were strong, of course, but when their week was over and she left, surely that dazzle would dim and she'd learn to refocus on other things.

She had to believe it.

Hours later Lina paused in a fragrant palace courtyard on the way back to her room, her mind full of Sayid.

Though they'd travelled back to the palace together, he'd left her in the grand foyer, heading towards his office. She shouldn't have been surprised. He never accompanied her on the long walk to their adjoining suites, even if they left an official function at the same time. It was as if he didn't want to remind anyone that they stayed alone together at one end of the palace complex.

Was he protecting her reputation?

She should be grateful yet tonight she felt…on edge.

The need for Sayid swelled stronger than ever, drawing her skin tight and her nerves to a state of frantic anticipation.

Surely he'd come to her tonight. They hadn't spent a night apart since she'd taken up his proposition.

Heat eddied, slow and thick, through her pelvis.

That stare he'd sent her as she danced, so intense and brooding, had almost made her misstep. She'd wanted to go to him then, ignoring everyone. She'd wanted to make love with him, desperately. Wanted to feel his hands on her bare flesh, his hot breath against her lips, his powerful body moving in perfect harmony with hers.

Lina shivered and wrapped her arms around herself, sagging against a slender column in the arched colonnade surrounding the perfumed rose garden. Ordinarily she loved this place, but tonight found no peace here.

She wanted Sayid with every cell of her being. But she also craved the right to simply…be with him, not just when they had sex. She wanted a role in his life, and the thought petrified her.

Lina shook her head and turned towards her room. She couldn't afford to think like that. Their affair was time-limited and not negotiable.

Minutes later she opened the door to her rooms and entered the darkened space. Snicking the door shut

behind her she stepped forward and straight into the
looming figure that emerged from her sitting room.

'Sayid?' The word ended in a muffled sound of
pleasure as his mouth slammed into hers, sealing her
lips.

Instantly desire rose like a whirlwind, blotting out
doubts and her earlier restless dissatisfaction.

This couldn't last but for now he was *hers*.

Throwing her arms around his neck, Lina fell into
him.

'Where the devil have you been?' he growled against
her mouth. 'I was going to send out a search party.'

Strong arms lashed her close, lifting her high till
her dancing slippers no longer touched the floor. She
adored his strength, his ability to make her feel at the
same time delicate yet powerful enough to match him.

Tunnelling her fingers through his thick hair she
nipped at his bottom lip, smiling at the low rumble
resonating at the back of his throat.

He moved, powering her across the space till she
felt something cool and hard at her shoulders. Disori-
entated, Lina opened her eyes and realised they were
in her sitting room, up against the reinforced glass
door that led onto her balcony.

Pressed between Sayid and the door, she curled her
leg up, hitching it around his hip. A shudder racked
her as the move brought her up against his erection.
Her need for him, for the affirmation of his lovemaking, escalated to impossible heights. It took only
that, his mouth and his body against hers and she was
lost…desperate.

Holding tight, she tried to climb higher, but was
frustrated by her dress. The skirt wasn't wide enough.

A whimper escaped just as one big hand closed over her breast, sending a spasm of pleasure rocketing through her.

Seconds later dark eyes snared hers. For a moment Lina gazed into his proud face. Then there was a whirl of movement as Sayid gripped her waist and put her down. Thankfully he held her as he spun her around, or she'd have lost her balance.

Dazed, Lina stared through the glass at the city lights spread like glittering jewels across the dark plain before them. Then the sprinkle of lights blurred as Sayid tugged her long skirt high, baring her legs and hips. Cool air rushed around her bare flesh and she shivered, surprised at how exposed she felt, though she still wore all her clothes. But then her dress was rucked up to her hips.

Her heightened senses discerned the familiar musky scent of arousal sharp in the air. The sound of laboured breathing, and, she closed her eyes in thankfulness, the rasp of a zip.

Her blood pounded as Sayid slid his hand onto her hip then delved forward to the flimsy fabric of her panties.

Lina's breath stopped on a gasp at his sharp tug and the sound of tearing fabric.

'Sayid?' But whatever she'd been going to say died as he kissed her, open-mouthed and hungry, on the sensitive spot at the base of her neck, while his long fingers slid low through the damp curls between her legs. Instantly she opened her legs wider, winning a husky sound of approval. Then that questing hand slid further and she arched into his touch.

'You want me, little one?'

Lina nodded, her voice locked somewhere in her throat. She opened her mouth but only managed a sound of raw pleasure as his fingers flirted with the sensitive bud.

'I've wanted *you* all day.' Sayid nipped at her neck then pressed an open-mouthed kiss there, sending fiery trails through her blood. 'I wanted you at the wedding when you danced for all those other men.'

Lina was about to say she'd danced for him and no one else, but he spoke again. 'I wanted to march over there and claim you, drag you off and have my way with you.' His voice was ragged and sharp with need. A need she felt as he pressed his erection against her bare buttocks. Instantly Lina braced herself on the window, pushing back towards all that inviting heat.

'You can have me now,' she whispered, her own voice thready. Lina had no pride, no desire to hold back, when she wanted exactly what he did.

'I can, can't I?' Pleasure rang in his husky voice as he clamped her hips and jerked her back against him. It was what she wanted but it wasn't nearly enough.

Lina circled her pelvis, needing more contact, and felt him jolt in response. Seconds later heat nudged between her legs, resolving into the press of his erection probing, then pushing further till she snatched a shaky breath, wondering at the sense of being utterly possessed.

'Easy, little one. It's all right.'

She needed to catch her breath, grow accustomed to this powerful invasion that filled her to the brim in the most wonderful way. Yet even as the thought surfaced, Sayid moved, withdrawing then surging back again with a force that expelled a soft breath from her lips.

One hand left her hip to capture her breast and Lina couldn't stifle the moan of pleasure rising in her throat. It coincided with his next thrust and she found herself arching hard to meet it.

In the distance the city lights dissolved into a blur, then disappeared altogether as his other hand arrowed down her belly to press on the nub at the centre of her desire.

Just then Sayid thrust hard again and everything rose within her, exploding in a shattering climax that splintered her soul and festooned the darkness with shards of radiance more brilliant than any city lights.

He rose high within her, then she felt the heavy, desperate pulse as he spilled himself in ecstasy, heard his sharp cry of triumph, and lost herself just as his arms folded around her, drawing her flush against him.

The rest of the night was like that. Intervals of desperate desire and radiant delight interspersed with quieter moments of incredible closeness.

It was as if an unseen barrier had fractured, Lina pondered drowsily as she lay, eyes closed, smiling while Sayid traced her body with light fingertips. He'd said he was a passionate, demanding man, but she'd never realised exactly what that meant before. Or how much she revelled in his earthy, carnal nature.

It was as if, in responding to him, Lina had discovered a new facet to her femininity. A readiness for whatever erotic delight Sayid wanted.

Because she too had a strongly sensual nature? Or was it more—was it because this was Sayid?

Lina shivered and instantly that caressing hand paused. 'I'm sorry. I've kept you awake. You need your sleep. You've got time before breakfast.'

As he said it, she felt him move away across the bed.

'Sayid?' She opened her eyes to discover it was day, early rays of light spilling across the room.

'Shh. Sleep while I shower.' He pressed a kiss to her hand then straightened, so magnificent with his tall, muscled form that Lina simply stared, arrested. Even now his powerful masculine beauty undid her.

Then, before she could protest, he was gone, leaving her wishing for more.

Not just more sex. But wishing for things that were impossible.

CHAPTER ELEVEN

DELIBERATELY SAYID TOOK his time in the bathroom, showering, shaving and donning fresh clothes. Lina needed sleep. He'd kept her awake through the night. Desperation had clawed at him, a need to sate himself on her before their allotted time ended.

Day six. He had today and tomorrow—that was all. *Unless he renegotiated with Lina.*

Surely that would be no problem. She was as avid for him as he was for her.

No, the difficulty was the precedent it would set, admitting that for the first time ever his self-imposed boundaries had shifted and he needed more from a woman. He could see no end to wanting Lina.

All his life he'd devoted himself to duty as a warrior then as leader, putting others first, except in those short intervals he permitted himself to enjoy a lover. Lina threatened to disrupt the balance he'd worked so hard to maintain.

He pushed the door to the bedroom open, assuring himself he was inflating the issue. They'd had spectacular sex. That was all. He made complications where there were none.

Sayid halted as a haunting melody reached him,

a pure voice softly singing. Lina's voice was as true as any he'd heard and he responded to the longing he heard in her words. He wanted to reach out and comfort her, make her smile.

She sat gilded by light near the window, her head bent, hair spilling in lustrous waves to her waist. She wore a loose wrap and clearly she was naked beneath it. He calculated he could strip her out of it in seconds.

Lina looked up at his approach, a smile lighting her face, and something smacked him in the chest. It wasn't just her beauty but her welcome that made her glow, as if she was lit from within just seeing him.

An answering warmth flared inside.

'What are you singing?' Curiously, his voice was husky.

Her smile faded. 'Just an old tune from home.'

'I've never heard it,' he said, for some reason needing to rationalise its haunting power. 'What's it about, apart from moonlight?'

Lina shrugged, her breasts rising against the shimmery fabric. 'The woman's lover has gone far away. She pines for him, wondering if he'll return as he'd promised. But she takes comfort from the moon, knowing no matter how far away he is, and even if she can never embrace him again, they share its light.'

Abruptly she looked away and he realised she was discomfited. Why? He moved nearer.

'You have a beautiful voice.'

Her head jerked back. 'You think so?'

'Absolutely.' He frowned. 'You didn't know?' Yet he read nothing but startled pleasure in her expression. And…was that guilt?

'I don't…' Again the lift of a shoulder. 'I was never

encouraged to sing after my mother died, or dance. My father, and then my aunt and uncle, said I shouldn't remind people that my mother had been a paid entertainer. They believed it reflected badly on me.'

Fury brewed in Sayid's belly. He saw hurt cloud Lina's eyes before she swiftly veiled them with long lashes. Was her family really so warped they believed something so simple and joyous was proof of moral weakness?

'You have a beautiful voice and it's a pleasure to watch you dance.'

Again that shrug. 'The wedding dance was the first time I've danced in years, but I couldn't resist.'

'You should do it more often if it makes you happy.' Sayid's jaw was tight, his teeth clenched as he thought of his vibrant lover, stifling herself because singing and dancing were deemed immoral.

'What else makes you happy, Lina?' He sank onto a nearby chair and leaned forward, forearms on his knees, thoroughly intrigued. He knew Lina, but suddenly he wanted to know much more.

She met his eyes and blushed, making him laugh as delight coiled. 'Apart from sex.' He rejoiced in their shared hunger.

The blush intensified. 'Talking to people, learning about their lives.'

That didn't surprise him. He'd seen the way she'd bridged the gap between herself and foreign businesspeople, and local townsfolk, even his private secretary, to become fast friends. 'What else?'

'Languages. Stories.' She paused, then reading his intent expression continued, this time lowering her head to what she held in her lap. 'Sewing. Little children. Dogs. I'm quite ordinary and domestic.'

She said it dismissively. Sayid couldn't work out why.

Domesticity wasn't something he'd thought about. Yet in the shared silence of early morning, watching Lina pick up a needle and begin sewing again, Sayid felt an unfamiliar tranquillity, reminding him of the peace he'd known as a young child. His days and nights were crammed with work responsibilities. It was rare simply to sit and chat because he wanted to, not in his role as national leader.

Sayid sank back in his chair, wondering how much of that peace stemmed from Lina's presence. 'What are you doing? Is that my shirt?'

'It is. You tore it last night.' A smile tugged at her lips, but she didn't look up. 'Either you were too energetic in the archery, or riding, or…' her smile grew '…undressing.'

'You don't need to mend it.' He watched the needle flash with her quick, precise movements.

'It's just a small tear. Besides, I enjoy sewing.'

'It's not a chore?' Sayid leaned back in his seat, fascinated. Who'd have thought the sexy siren who'd tormented him so long was a devoted needlewoman?

'I don't enjoy fine needlework. My aunt will tell you my embroidery is dreadful. But mending or making clothes I don't mind. I make all my dresses.'

Sayid stared, remembering the gowns that had seemed demure but which, with their figure-hugging contours, were a delectable sight.

'What?' She looked up, as if sensing his surprise.

'You made the dresses you've worn in the palace?'

Her chin lifted. 'I thought they looked good.'

Good! He hadn't been able to take his eyes off her.

'Better than good.' He shook his head. 'I'd never have guessed. But surely your allowance covers—'

'I *liked* sewing them. And I bought the fabric with money I saved when I was away.' She paused. 'Now that I've finished my schooling I prefer not to take an allowance from you. It's enough that I'm staying here in the palace.'

Sayid's stare hardened. It wasn't that he didn't believe her. He did. It was easy to read the determined set of her jaw and the challenging light in her eyes.

How many people would relinquish financial support?

He thought of previous lovers who'd been only too happy to accept jewels and expensive clothes. Lina accepted nothing but the roof over her head. She'd made a point of her determination to pay him back for the education he'd organised.

As if satisfied that he wasn't going to argue, Lina turned back to her sewing.

He should leave. He had meetings to prepare for. Instead Sayid sat, well-being like a hum in his blood.

'What's that?' He gestured to a box covered in tiny beads fashioned into a profusion of flowers.

Lina followed his glance, her hand closing around the box. 'A sewing case my mother made.' And precious, Sayid had no doubt, noting how her fingers lingered on it.

'You were close to her.'

Lina's smile was wistful. 'She was everything to me. Friend and mother too. My father was…distant.

She encouraged me to believe the world could be wonderful.'

It was something Lina had definitely absorbed. People automatically responded to her vibrant personality. *He* responded.

'I should go.' Yet he didn't move, just watched her snip the thread and hold up his shirt to inspect it. There was something about sitting here with her, sharing this quiet time that made him feel…good. Refreshed.

'What do you like, Sayid?'

'Sorry?' She closed her sewing box and sat, watching him.

'What makes you happy?' She paused, a tiny smile flirting with the corners of her mouth. 'Apart from sex.'

He huffed out a laugh. 'Meetings that end on time. Provincial governors who govern well.'

Lina shook her head. 'I mean personally. What do you enjoy?'

Enjoy? Sayid hadn't thought about personal pleasure in years, apart from brief sexual encounters. 'A ruler hasn't time for enjoyment.'

'Surely not. Even kings and prime ministers have hobbies.'

Hobbies? Sayid shook his head. 'Not this ruler. I inherited a country on the brink of war. A country that hadn't altered appreciably in a generation. It's taken a lot of effort from many people to turn Halarq from a nation primed for war to one ready for a peaceful future.' He crossed his ankles, pride warming his belly. They'd come a long way.

'Plus I wasn't born to this role, so I've had to learn fast. My cousin was groomed for the position but he died a year before my uncle.' Meningitis had struck so fast, he'd been hale and hearty one day and dead the next.

'I'm sorry.' Lina tilted her head as if to view him better. 'Were you close?'

Sayid shrugged. 'Only as children. We hadn't seen much of each other in years.'

While Sayid was a soldier, protecting the country, his cousin had pursued a life of luxury, delighting in the perks of his position and his ability to get any woman he wanted. Would he have turned into a copy of his father? The signs had been there, signs Sayid had vowed not to emulate. Instead Sayid modelled himself on his own father, a decent, honourable man.

The whisper of silk on flesh caught Sayid's attention and he saw Lina reach out as if to touch him. Instantly she sat back, her hand dropping to her lap.

Because of his frown? Or because, despite being lovers, he was still her Emir?

Suddenly he was aware of the gap between them, the one he conveniently ignored when they shared their bodies. Discontent stirred. He was tired of that unseen barrier between him and everyone else. Why couldn't he be close, genuinely close to someone? Why did there always have to be this distance?

Yet Lina, being Lina, wasn't as daunted as others might have been. She held his gaze, eyebrows arching. 'So you've been busy. But you're a man as well as a head of state. What is it that makes you happy?'

Sayid felt amusement tug at his lips. She really was unlike anyone else he knew. 'Solving problems,' he said without thinking. 'Finding innovative ways to do things.'

Lina nodded. 'That's one of the reasons you're so good at government.' She said it as casually as if assessing his performance as Emir were the norm. 'What else?'

'Sport. Archery and team sports. I loved football in my teens and dreamed of becoming a professional, but that wasn't an option.' The nephew of Halarq's Emir must serve the Crown, not do anything as frivolous as make a living kicking a ball.

'Do you miss football?'

For a second Sayid considered, then shook his head. 'It was fun but I prefer the challenges I've got now.' He'd never thought of it that way, but it was true. His current role was never boring.

'So, you like sex, solving problems and sport. That's all?' She looked so expectant that Sayid didn't want to disappoint her. He thought for a moment then smiled. 'And astronomy.' He waggled his eyebrows. 'Come to my room tonight and I'll show you my big telescope. It's very large and powerful.'

Lina burst into laughter, the sound a rich, infectious peal, making him chuckle. 'I bet you say that to all the women.'

She looked so…pretty when she smiled at him like that. Gorgeous, yes. Sexy, of course. But…pretty and appealing too in a way that had nothing to do with sex appeal, or almost nothing. Sayid had never known a woman like her. Would he ever tire of discovering new facets to her?

'No, it's true! I do have a powerful telescope.' His lips twitched as she giggled again and slanted a look towards his groin. Instantly he felt the tight, hot swell of arousal. When she came to his room tonight they wouldn't be looking at the stars, even if he did ask his staff to locate the telescope that had been packed away for years.

'I'd like you to tell me about the stars. I don't even know their names.'

'The best place to see them is the desert, away from city lights.' And just like that Sayid found himself planning to take Lina into the desert. There was a spot he'd camped in the old days, perfect for stargazing. After that—

'Is that the time?' Catching sight of his watch, Lina jumped up in a flurry of silk and curves, making his belly contract at the glimpses of toned thigh and bare breast. 'I'm supposed to be meeting Leonor in an hour. Senhora Neves,' she explained, tugging her robe close and depriving him of his view.

'Then you'd better leave.' Sayid got to his feet and wrapped an arm around Lina's waist. Instantly she stilled, leaning into him.

Yes. That was better. Lina in his arms. He bent and kissed her full on the lips, possessing her mouth in a languorous yet purposeful caress that made her slump against him, arms around his neck. She kissed him back with an enthusiasm that threatened to seduce him from his own schedule.

Finally, breathing deep, he put her from him, pleased at her moue of regret. 'I'll let you go first.' Though they each left from their own suites, he made a point of never entering or leaving his private wing with Lina. There was no reason to court speculation about their relationship. 'I've got a briefing to read before my first meeting.'

Even so, Sayid registered regret when she left. He'd

enjoyed simply talking with Lina, laughing and for a while being just a man, enjoying the companionship of a beautiful, intriguing woman.

Tonight he'd talk to her about their arrangement. Clearly seven days wouldn't be enough for either of them.

Thirty minutes later Sayid left his chambers. Turning a corner into a colonnaded courtyard he paused, recognising the lush rose scent he associated with Lina. Had she just passed this way or was the perfume from the roses in the courtyard?

'She's so beautiful. And nice too. Not many VIPs stop to say hello to a cleaner.' The woman's voice came from the shadows further down the colonnade.

'Of course she's beautiful.' This voice, older and irascible, was male. 'She's the Emir's concubine, here to warm his bed. You don't think he'd accept an ugly woman for sex, do you?'

'Concubine?' No mistaking the amazement in the woman's voice. 'That can't be right. You don't mean—?'

'I mean she was sent here to spread her legs for His Highness. He didn't want her then and sent her off to get a little more gloss and, if you ask me, more experience of men so she could service him better. But fancy manners and rich clothes don't make her better than any other whore—'

'Silence!' Sayid's voice cut like a lash, ripping with the force of his fury. The two staff members, cleaning ornate hanging lanterns, whipped round, dismayed. 'Report to your supervisor now. I'll contact him shortly. You—' he pointed to the elder one, a sour-faced man, now cringing '—will be looking for a new job.'

The woman had done no wrong but would have to be reminded about the need for confidentiality regarding what she saw and heard in the palace. As for the man… Sayid would like to throw him personally into one of the old dungeons beneath the citadel.

They scuttled off, bowing out backwards, but that did nothing to dampen Sayid's white-hot ire.

To hear Lina described like that!

He stalked the length of the colonnade then swung back, fist pounding his palm.

He'd known there'd be some people in the palace who remembered her arrival years ago. But the construction that lowlife had put on her time overseas, that she'd been sent away to acquire the skills of a whore—

Sayid swung round and slammed his hand against a marble pillar, relishing physical pain as a distraction from the ferocious agony as something inside tore asunder.

His conscience?

He'd known Lina's reputation would suffer if she became his lover. But that hadn't stopped him. He'd been intent on his own pleasure.

She'd been the one at his beck and call. What right had he to seduce the woman who'd been sent to him as an innocent girl? The woman he *knew* felt indebted to him!

The woman whose name and chance of ever finding a decent Halarqi husband one day would be destroyed if such stories got out.

Swearing, Sayid stalked down the side of the court-

yard, then back again and again, seeking a way to protect Lina. Knowing whatever he did it was too late.
The damage was done.

An hour ago he'd bragged that he liked solving
problems. Now he needed to be innovative to redress
a wrong *he'd* caused.

Bile seared his throat.

The cleaner might have said the words but it was
Sayid who'd done the damage. Times might have
changed yet Halarqi society would be unrelenting in
its disapproval of a woman it saw as his whore. Look
at how Lina's mother had been treated, just because
she'd been a dancer.

He'd been pacing the corridor for a lifetime it
seemed when the answer came to him. So simple, so
effective, it hit him like a flash of lightning. Sayid's
mouth curved into a taut, hard smile. Relief surged,
and determination.

He swung round and strode to his office. He had
arrangements to make.

'You wanted to see me?' Lina did her best to sound
nonchalant, but her heart tripped over itself. Sayid
never sent for her. He went out of his way to maintain
the appearance of distance between them.

Yet this morning as she'd sat sewing, they'd talked
and, she couldn't explain it, but something had
changed. *He'd* changed. She'd sensed a softening, an
understanding that surely had been about more than
sex.

Perhaps Sayid would suggest they share more than
her allotted week. Because he'd begun to feel…

Her gaze fixed on Sayid, standing by the window of his library, staring over the sprawling city. His hands were behind his back and his feet planted wide. His strong jaw was tight, his brow furrowed.

Was she kidding herself? That indefinable shift between them—had she been the only one to feel it? Had it been imagination? Or worse, wishful thinking?

'Yes. Come in, please.' His eyes met hers, their dark glitter sending inevitable tremors through her. They were alone yet Lina couldn't read his expression. It wasn't desire, nor anything as tender as she thought she'd seen earlier. As for shared laughter… definitely not.

Whatever the reason he'd sent for her, it was serious.

Lina crossed the room, halting a few steps away. Even now, alone in a room where no one, not even his secretary, would interrupt without knocking, Sayid kept his distance. Lina's smile froze in place.

Had she really expected him to haul her close like he did when they were in his quarters? Then they were Lina and Sayid. But everywhere else, they were Emir and subject, guardian and ward.

Lina linked her hands before her and waited, telling herself it didn't matter that he didn't embrace her.

Lying to herself as usual.

She didn't know how much longer she could play this game of pretending not to care. Not when she cared too much, wanted too much.

She forced herself to speak, since Sayid seemed to be brooding on his own thoughts.

'And you wanted to see me because…?'

A skewed smile lifted his mouth at one corner. 'No one else speaks to me the way you do. Do you know that?'

Lina swallowed the retort that she hoped not. She was his lover after all. Instead she merely tilted her head questioningly.

'It's about our…arrangement,' he said finally.

She couldn't help it. Her heart leapt. This morning she'd believed he shared some of the emotional attachment she felt. Now, staring up at his still features, the idea seemed ridiculous, yet hope lingered. Perhaps he *was* going to admit he wanted her to stay longer. And if she stayed longer, who knew what might happen?

'Yes?' She licked suddenly dry lips and Sayid's gaze dropped to the movement. The air thickened. Or was that her heart labouring?

'It's no longer appropriate.' His hands flexed at his sides and Lina sensed he held himself still despite a strong urge for action.

'Not appropriate?' Her voice was anything but even.

Her heart pounded right up in her throat. Excitement soared despite her stern attempts to stay calm. Did he feel what she did? Was it possible Sayid had begun to care for her? Not as a ward or a responsibility, but as his love?

She pressed her lips together, waiting. She sensed her future happiness rested on his words.

'That's right.' He smiled down at her but curiously, Lina didn't read happiness in his expression, just determination. 'I want you to marry me.'

CHAPTER TWELVE

THEY WERE WORDS she'd never thought to hear. Yet she'd dreamed of them. They reverberated through her whole being. Lina's pulse pounded an ecstatic rhythm.

But even as her body buzzed with the intense rush of awed delight, she stood, rooted to the floor. For something wasn't right. Sayid's stance, his tone, his expression, didn't ring true.

On the verge of tumbling forward into his arms, Lina stopped herself, frozen in place like her lover.

He didn't look like her lover now. There was no desire in his eyes, no smile, either indulgent or predatory. No warmth.

Definitely no love.

He looked hard and unemotional. Determined and ruthless. Even a little fierce.

Lina rocked back on her heels, swallowing the scratchy mass of emotion blocking her throat. It didn't take intuition to know something was wrong.

Yet it took everything she had not to go to him, rest her head on his wide chest and say yes.

If she closed her eyes and concentrated on his words she might convince herself this was the beginning of her happy ever after. Only for a moment. Sayid looked so rigid the illusion shattered.

'Why?'

'Sorry?' Grooves lined his forehead as if no one had ever questioned him before. Maybe they hadn't since he became Emir.

'Why do you want me to marry you?'

Blank eyes stared down at her and Lina's nape prickled as every fine hair stood erect in premonition. Whatever this was, it wasn't good.

'Isn't it enough that I want it?' Surprise flashed in his eyes and hauteur laced his tone. Those aristocratic features tightened and apprehension washed through her. Sayid wasn't only her lover but her ruler. A man with the power to change her life for ever.

But he'd already done that. He'd set her free.

Lina met his eyes steadily despite the staccato rattle of her heart and the desperate heave of lungs that couldn't drag in enough oxygen.

'I didn't know you were thinking of marriage.' She'd heard whispers that the elders were talking about the need for a royal heir, but the consensus was that Sayid had no inclination to marry yet.

One dark eyebrow rose as if in surprise at her temerity. 'Yet I am.' He paused and seemed to gather himself. This time his smile almost reached his eyes. 'I want you as my wife.'

Again the urge to fall into his embrace was almost irresistible. It would have been, Lina knew, if he'd opened his arms. She was strong but not that strong. Instead he held himself still, watching her with something in his eyes—detachment or calculation—that made her spine crackle as it iced over.

'Is it because you forgot to use a condom last night? Are you afraid I might be pregnant?'

He stiffened, a real feat when he was already ramrod straight. His mouth twisted wryly. 'I hoped you hadn't noticed. I didn't want you to worry. It was appalling of me to forget.'

Relief poured through Lina and some of the tension left her taut frame. She'd found his unstoppable passion anything but appalling.

'I wasn't worried.' Secretly she'd wondered if it might be possible his child was even now forming inside her. It was stupid to think it, since the chances were slim. Yet that hadn't stopped the glow of delight that had carried her through the day. 'I knew you'd look after me, if I got pregnant.'

Lina paused, watching Sayid's face, knowing there was more. She could take the proposal at face value or she could probe. Perhaps the fact there hadn't actually *been* a proposal was what made her persist.

'The chances are I'm not pregnant.' Her voice dipped on the last word. 'A marriage would be premature.'

Why was she holding back when she wanted this so much?

Because she wanted Sayid to want her in the same way. Yet he looked anything but jubilant or excited.

He scowled. 'You don't *want* to marry me?' Disbelief made his voice rise. If the situation weren't so fraught Lina might have smiled. Her lover was so absolutely sure of himself, and with good reason.

'What I want, Sayid, is to know why you want to marry me.' She folded her arms across her chest, hoping to look stronger than she felt despite the yearning to say yes. 'We've always been honest with each other. I'd like to understand.' When still he remained silent she continued quickly. 'It's not as if you love me.'

If this were her fantasy he'd pull her to him and admit he was crazy with love for her. That it didn't matter that she was from another class, ill-suited for the role of Sheikha. That he cared for nothing but her.

Dream on, Lina.

Nevertheless, she was on tenterhooks waiting for his reply.

'Royalty doesn't marry for love, Lina.' For the first time since she'd entered the room she saw a flash of the man she'd fallen for. The man who, love or not, cared for her, at least a little. The warmth in his eyes spoke of tenderness and—

She sucked in a sharp breath, sure that was pity she read in his expression.

'I understand that,' she said quickly. 'That's why I'm surprised. I'm hardly an appropriate royal bride.'

Instantly he moved nearer, then pulled up abruptly, as if preferring to keep his distance. The chill that had started in her spine worked inwards towards her vital organs. No, he wasn't overcome by love.

'You underestimate yourself, Lina. You're beautiful and charming. You have winning ways and would make an excellent hostess. Given time I'm sure the people will love you.'

The people, but not Sayid. It was what he *didn't* say that spoke most loudly.

'It's true my advisers have been pointing out the advantages of a royal marriage to secure the throne for the future.'

A baby. That was what he meant. The pair of them

making a baby together. Lina's arms tightened protectively around her body at the sudden uprush of excitement at the idea of becoming a mother to Sayid's child.

Yet her excitement soured. She might be a country girl, still learning the ways of the city, she might be late acquiring an education, but some things she understood. She knew the reality of an unequal marriage.

Lina didn't want a marriage like her parents' where all power rested with the husband and the wife was expected to be continually grateful he'd plucked her out of poverty. She didn't want a marriage solely to beget an heir.

She wanted a man who'd be her partner, even if to the outside world his authority far outstripped hers. She wanted to be able to speak her mind, help make decisions and above all love and be loved in return.

You don't want much, do you? See where your western education with its ideas of equality between the sexes has left you?

'Still,' she persisted, wondering where she found the strength to withstand not only Sayid but her own reckless heart, 'you don't need to marry me. A few days will confirm if I'm pregnant.' Her eyes narrowed on his sombre features. 'Something has happened, hasn't it? What?'

'Isn't it enough that I want this?'

This. Not you.

Suddenly revelation hit. Lina had her answer. It *wasn't* enough.

Because she loved him. She'd been in love since she was seventeen and instead of growing out of it, she'd fallen deeper in love with Sayid.

She loved him and wanted his love in return. It might be hopeless, ridiculous, asking the impossible of the man who'd already given her so much, but that was what she craved. Lina was no longer subservient enough to be overawed by him. Or to settle for a relationship where she wasn't valued. Sayid had taught her to value herself and she couldn't go back to being a chattel.

'Why, Sayid?'

'No one else pushes the boundaries like you. You know that, don't you?' He crossed his arms, echoing her stance, yet on him it looked combative not protective. Finally he spoke. 'Because it's the right thing.'

His jaw firmed and his pulse beat hard at his temple. He looked on the edge of losing his temper, something she'd never seen.

'Because I was a virgin?' But if that were the case surely they'd have had this conversation days ago.

His head jerked back as if she'd slapped him. She even thought he paled.

'That too.' He nodded. 'You deserve a respectable outcome.'

A respectable outcome. It sounded so impersonal, as if she were a business or a government strategy. Not a woman craving warmth and love.

Nausea rose from her belly to her mouth, acid burning her throat.

'Something's happened. Someone has said I'm *not* respectable—is that it?'

His slashing gesture was all repressed violence, the light in his eyes furious. 'It doesn't matter. There was a little…talk but it's been contained. You don't need to worry about it.'

Lina stumbled a little, saw him lunge towards her and shoved out her arm, palm out, holding him at bay. 'Don't. Please.' She sidestepped to one of the heavy chairs, her fingers clawing the carved back like talons, needing its support. 'I'm fine.'

Now things made sense. Sayid's abrupt decision to marry. His air of resolve, like a man bent on doing his duty, no matter how unpalatable.

Because he saw *her* as a duty.

Her stomach plummeted in a freefall that hollowed her insides. How long before duty morphed into resentment? If, because of her, he had to change his life?

She looked into those serious eyes, narrowed as if trying to read her thoughts. Sayid was bent on doing the right thing. He was a decent man, he even cared enough to want to protect her. That in itself was remarkable.

Lina knew she could ask for no more. It was lunacy to ask for love when she could have marriage to Sayid.

Clearly she was mad, for she couldn't, *wouldn't* force him to marry her in such circumstances.

She loved him too much to shackle him to her when his heart wasn't engaged. Lina imagined the years passing, he growing ever more dissatisfied but determined to put up with his unsuitable bride and she losing the self-respect she'd worked so hard to acquire. If they were lucky there might be children. Her heart ached for those children. She imagined it breaking all over again if the best Sayid could do was his duty to the children of his low-born wife, rather than love them.

She blinked to clear her blurred vision, her gaze colliding with his.

'Thank you, Sayid. I appreciate that you're will-ing to do so much for me.' The ache inside welled so high she had to force the words out through a throat that worked convulsively. 'But the answer is no. I can't marry you.'

Sayid stared, reading emotion in Lina's over-bright eyes.

Yet it was nothing to the slam of astonishment that rocked him back on his heels.

She couldn't marry him?

She was *sorry*?

Not good enough, Lina! Totally unacceptable, in fact.

Did she have any concept of the honour he be-stowed? He thought of the royal princesses and wealthy, sophisticated women who vied for his at-tention, who'd accept whatever terms he set to be-come his wife.

And little Lina Rahman, who'd come to the palace as his servant, his *slave*, demurred?

Fire blasted him, searing his belly, coursing through his veins, burning his retinas as a red mist of fury de-scended.

She was his lover. She shared her body willingly, no *ardently*, as if she had but one thought—to make him happy. And she had. Supremely, breathtakingly happy. He'd never felt as good as he had this week. Even interminable negotiations and royal red tape dissolved into inconveniences to be laughed off at the prospect of bedding Lina again. Of simply being with her.

He'd seen the dazzled look in her eyes, registered

the needy way she clung to him, even if she never put that neediness into words or demands for his time. She was the perfect lover in fact. Passionate, sensual, generous. Attuned to his needs even, he realised with a stir of disquiet, when he hadn't known what he'd needed. Like this morning when he'd found peace in her quiet conversation. Like the other times she'd chivvied him into laughter and he'd realised how little time he'd had for humour.

Like the times, after sex, when instead of pulling away because he didn't do post-coital cuddles, he'd let her enfold him in her slender arms, stroke his heaving back or thread her fingers through his hair and he'd discovered he wanted those moments of tenderness as much as she!

A shudder racked him. Annoyance, he told himself. Indignation.

'You presume too much,' he bit out. 'It wasn't a question. I've decided we'll marry.' He'd brook no argument.

Those violet eyes sparked, reminding him of thunderstorms over the mountains and the savage lightning strikes that did such damage in that wild landscape.

'You've decided, so I'm supposed to agree.'

Sayid nodded. 'It's for the best. For you.' Couldn't she see he did this to protect her?

Her chin jerked up as if pulled by a string and she let go of the chair. Her hands rammed down onto her hips. She was ridiculous, trying to defy him, for she was doomed to defeat. Yet she looked stunning. Like some haughty princess of old, demanding obedience.

It hit him that far from being unsuitable as a royal

wife, Lina was perfect. She wasn't a burden but an asset, publicly and in private. He defied anyone to find a woman who'd be better for him and his people.

'You can't just command me to marry you!' The mulish set of her lovely mouth and the obstinate angle of her jaw said this wasn't Lina being coy.

Sayid frowned, scrubbing a hand around the back of his neck where the muscles drew so tight, a headache began to throb.

For the first time he wished he knew how women thought. He'd been content with perfectly satisfying, albeit shallow relationships. His liaisons were for physical release, not for sharing souls. He hadn't a clue what motivated Lina.

His was a man's world. He'd loved his mother, but from an early age he'd focused on learning and living up to his father's warrior code. At fifteen, soon after his father's death, he'd become a man, defending his mother from rape and forced marriage. His mother had died soon after, of a broken heart, some said.

Which meant he'd spent almost half his life with no women close to him. No sisters or aunts. No woman who could unpick the intricacies and absurdities of the female mind. For Lina's refusal was nothing short of absurd.

How could she not want to marry him?

A stray thought filled his mouth with bile. 'Is there someone else? Someone you want to—'

'No!' She looked so horrified relief filled him. For a moment there he'd wondered if she'd felt compelled to become his lover even though she cared for someone else. Nausea still swirled in his belly.

He hadn't compelled her. She'd been free to choose.

And there was no mistaking her enjoyment of what they did together.

Yet a seed of doubt lingered. When she'd come to the palace originally she'd been morally if not legally too young to choose a lover. He'd done the right thing, sending her away, keeping his hands off her. Sayid told himself she was now an independent woman who'd *chosen* to accept an affair. But was there a chance that she'd felt…obliged to take him into her bed?

His gut churned in horror.

Sayid refused to believe it. Lina had learned to say no. Look at her now, all defiance and pride. Yet he knew he could sweep her into his arms and persuade her.

But that shred of doubt stopped him. He couldn't bear even the tiniest possibility she'd given him sex out of gratitude. Or out of coercion. Which made it all the more imperative he right the wrong he'd done her, putting her reputation in danger. They must marry!

Yet his honour demanded she come to him freely.

It was time to be magnanimous. 'I've rushed you. I know it's a surprise. I'll leave you to digest the idea.' He even conjured a smile, though his facial muscles felt stretched taut. She probably just needed reassurance. 'But it will work out, you'll see. You'll make a fine Sheikha.'

'I'm sorry, Sayid. But I'm not marrying you.' Her hands were clasped before her now. She looked so damned *earnest*.

Impatience rose. Sayid had never been rejected in his life. It was impossible he'd be refused now. He turned and marched across the room then back again, needing an outlet for the tide of furious energy that made him want to grab her and kiss her into submission.

Only his promise to himself that he wouldn't coerce her stopped him. Frustration tore at him, yet he forced himself to keep his distance, just. He stopped out of touching distance, his breath laboured at the effort of restraint, his temper spiking at her obstinacy.

Lina stood there in one of her western dresses, lilac this time, looking sexy and seductive and mutinous and he wanted to kiss her mouth till it softened, strip her bare and stake his claim over that glorious body in the most primitive, definite way possible. He was aroused just watching the quick rise and fall of her breasts and the flare of emotion in her bright stare.

That enraged him even more than her refusal. She stood there, not calm, but at least self-possessed, saying no, and he felt utterly adrift, as if every tie that tethered him to the real world had been ripped away.

He prowled towards her, in the grip of an unholy mix of hunger, indignation and determination. Slowly he lifted his hand, watching her shiver in anticipation of his touch. He brushed his knuckle down her cheek and the shiver became a shudder, her tight mouth opening on a silent gasp of delight.

Satisfaction thundered through him.

If there'd been any question that Lina hadn't shared this sexual obsession her reaction banished it. She quivered, leaning towards him as if needing more than that light touch.

Sayid's mouth turned up in a possessive smile as

his hand trailed from her chin to her throat then to her breast.

Lina's breath was a hiss then a sigh as he circled her nipple with one finger, feeling it peak beneath the fabric. Her breath came in uneven gasps and the pulse at her throat raced as quickly as his pounding blood. Deliberately he opened his palm, cupping her breast and gently squeezing. She pressed close as her eyelids fluttered low.

Still she refused to speak the words, though he knew she teetered on the brink of submission.

His body was on fire. His groin hard, hot and painfully tight. He could have her now on the chair behind her, or better yet, on the big desk. They both craved it. Craved each other.

Whether it was the realisation of how much he needed her or a remnant of his determination not to coerce, Sayid didn't know. But he found himself dropping his hand. Her eyes snapped open, velvety warm and bewildered and he had to step back rather than lose any hope of thought.

'Marriage is for the best, Lina.'

He watched her fight her way out of her sensual fog. It took a while, but he found little gratification in that since it took everything he had not to step in close again and let nature and their bodies do the thinking for them.

She shook her head. 'I've given you my answer, Sayid. Not that there was a question, much less a proposal.'

His eyebrows shot up. 'That's what this is about? You want me down on bended knee, proposing?'

She laughed and he didn't like the sound—so bitter. So unlike Lina. 'Frankly, I can't imagine you ever doing that.' She paused as if gathering herself. 'A proposal would have been nice but it wouldn't make a difference. I can't marry you.'

'Can't?' Fury turned his voice into a baritone growl. 'Or won't?'

She didn't even flinch. Just lifted her chin imperiously. 'Both.'

Sayid took a long step towards her, so close the ravishing scent of her skin clogged his senses, but he was beyond being seduced. Besides, *he* was the master at that. Once more he lifted his arm, reached out to her and stopped, his hand hovering so close to her breast he could almost feel it. The expression in her eyes confirmed her response to his phantom caress.

'You'll change your mind.' He took in her quickened pulse and the way she swayed towards him. Despite her rejection he caught the scent of female arousal as a musk undertone to that lavish rose scent. 'You're wet between the legs for me, aren't you, Lina?' Her glazed stare confirmed it. 'You want me right here, right now. You want the pleasure I can give you. *Only* I can give you. You want to come with me inside you. Or against my hand, or my mouth.'

Sayid's heart slammed against his ribcage in an urgent tattoo but he stood his ground, refusing to succumb to the need his own words evoked.

Lina swallowed hard and triumph buzzed in his veins. She shook like a leaf, trying to fight the inevitable.

'But know this. There will be no more sex until you agree to marry me. No more climaxes. No more kisses.' She gazed at him in disbelief. 'Nothing, until you say yes.'

Her breathing was a raw scratch of sound. Her cheeks flushed with an erotic heat he recognised. Just talking about climaxes aroused her. Lina was as highly sexed as he. She needed him. This, if nothing else, was her secret weakness and he had no qualms about exploiting it.

Sayid was congratulating himself on finding the perfect strategy for victory when Lina stunned him by stepping back. Her chest heaved and she clung once more to the chair back, but she stood there, staring up at him as if she'd never seen him before.

Something cold and hard sank in his belly.

'Then I'll just have to live without.' Her choked, uneven voice detracted from her defiance, but the look in her eyes told Sayid she was dead serious. She drew herself up to her full height. 'Thank you for the…consideration. I'm sorry I can't accept. I'll pack my bags and leave the palace.'

She turned and walked towards the door.

Away from him! Dismissing him and his honourable offer.

'Don't walk away from me!' His voice was a roar that filled the vast chamber. He who rarely raised his voice. 'I didn't give you permission to leave.'

She flinched, her shoulders lifting high, making him feel like a brute. Except that was ridiculous. He was her Sheikh and her lover. He deserved better.

Slowly Lina turned. When she did, instead of facing him with that determined, glittering gaze, she sank flat to the floor in an old-fashioned gesture of obeisance. The sort of thing he abhorred. The sort of servile gesture his autocratic uncle had loved.

Damn Lina. She did this deliberately. He was *not* turning into his uncle. Hadn't he given Lina the education she'd craved? A chance to experience the world beyond Halarq's borders?

And shown her too how to please a man. How to use her body for his pleasure.

Ice skated through him, freezing the fire in his veins.

Finally she looked up. Lina might be sprawled on the floor like some obedient courtier, but her eyes blazed.

'You don't really want me, Sayid. You just don't like being crossed. When you think it through you'll realise it's better if I go.'

Sayid's hands curled into fists that shook with the effort it took not to haul her up and over his shoulder.

How dare she tell him what he wanted? As if she knew best? He was doing this for *her*. Because what happened to her mattered to him. Yet she threw that back in his face!

'You may rise.' His voice was devoid of emotion. He refused to abase himself any further.

Lina rose from the carpet with a grace that only irked him.

'You may go.'

Was that a flash of hurt in her expression? Sayid couldn't be sure but it gave him hope, even as he felt a pang in response. He knew he'd prevail but he'd prefer to resolve this as soon as possible. He sighed. There'd be no resolution right now. Lina was so stubborn it would take a few hours at least, if not days for her to see what was before her eyes—that marriage was the ideal solution for them both.

'Don't pack your bags. You're not leaving the palace.'

She spun round in a swirl of skirts. His eyes dropped to her long, shapely legs then back up to her face.

'But it's best if I—'

'You agreed to work with the community liaison team to pay your debt to me.' He paused, watching her frown. 'Then you agreed to be my lover for seven days as an alternative.'

He waited for some sign that she understood the implications. When she didn't he went on, keeping his own features expressionless. 'We've only had five days together so the debt isn't paid.'

Lina opened her mouth as if to protest, then snapped it shut, her eyes narrowing on him. Sayid didn't care about her anger. What he cared about was getting what he wanted.

'Which means you still owe me for your education. I'll tell my staff you'll be working with them again in community liaison. We'll discuss later just how long it will take you to pay off the debt.'

He turned to his desk.

He had her now, he knew. Her honour wouldn't let her leave till she'd repaid the debt, even if she resented his devil's bargain. Given time Lina would see the wisdom of his scheme. And with her passionate nature it wouldn't be long before she was knocking on his door, begging him to make love to her. She might put on a fine show now but she wouldn't resist indefinitely.

Sayid hid a satisfied smile as he sat at his desk and looked towards the door.

Lina had gone. For there was nothing she could say, no argument she could make.

He'd won.

It was just a matter of waiting till she admitted it.

CHAPTER THIRTEEN

A DAY PASSED, then two. By the third day Sayid's smug-ness morphed into disquiet. Yet he didn't soften. He held all the aces and there was no way he'd relinquish his winning hand. Lina was *his*.

Three days became five, became a week and his patience frayed. Sleep eluded him, but for snatches just long enough for him to dream of Lina torturing him with her beautiful, bountiful body and her defi-ant attitude, teasing him then walking away, laughing as he fought to follow.

His patience with long-winded officials grew short, which bizarrely had the twofold consequence of mak-ing meetings more efficient and winning him respect from the elder statesmen who'd been wary of his at-tempts to achieve goals through consensus.

Pain throbbed constantly at the back of his skull because the muscles in his shoulders and neck refused to relax. Plus there was a low-grade ache in his belly he'd never had before. Fleetingly he wondered if it might be fear, except that was impossible. He was a soldier. He'd risked his life more than once.

Lina avoided him. The only time they'd come close was two days after his ultimatum in the library. She must have been waiting for him, for she appeared out of nowhere as he made his way to an audience with provincial leaders. She'd picked her time, as for once Makram, who usually accompanied him, was already in the audience chamber.

Sayid's heart had hit a triumphant beat as Lina sidled out from the arcade of pillars. He'd been sure she was there to capitulate.

Instead, eyes sombre, she'd sunk into one of those damnable deep curtseys as if she were a complete stranger, not his lover. When she rose her eyes looked dull and he'd wanted to pull her close. Never had he seen her look so listless.

'I just came to reassure you,' she'd said, her voice so low he had to lean in to catch it. 'I'm not pregnant.'

Then, as he opened his mouth to speak, she glided away so swiftly she was almost running.

Sayid was left gaping, unsure what he'd been going to say, suspecting it would have been words of tenderness. For despite his anger at her stubbornness, he hated seeing her distress.

Besides, it wasn't relief he felt at her news. It was loss. His belly clamped on regret.

Nor was it simply because pregnancy would make this simpler. He was sure Lina would agree to marry him if she carried his child.

No, it was because to his amazement he discovered he wanted a child with Lina!

He'd never particularly wanted a family before, though he knew it was his duty. Now the idea of children with Lina danced before him, tantalising and desirable.

At a visceral level Sayid wanted her pregnant with

his baby. He wanted to claim her, wanted all the world to know she was his and no one else's.

He'd made his way to the audience chamber and struggled through presentations and petitions. Thankfully his staff kept things moving when he lapsed more than once into distraction.

Now, a week after he'd invited Lina to marry him, Sayid had had enough. He'd been more patient than any other man would be in the circumstances. For he cared about her. He genuinely wanted her happy and safe.

Lina was in his blood, his mind, every minute of every hour. He *had* to resolve this.

He pushed open the door from his private courtyard into her apartment. At least she hadn't locked it against him.

It was so early she might still be in bed. Sayid told himself he hadn't chosen this time in the hope of finding her asleep and off guard, more vulnerable to…persuasion.

But she was awake, awake and dressed in a long robe that covered her from neck to ankles. Her eyes met his as she stepped out of the bathroom, hands yanking the belt tight around her waist.

'Sayid? What's wrong?'

His gaze ate her. From her glorious eyes to her hair cascading over her shoulders to her slim waist, right down to her bare feet that somehow seemed decadently sensual when the rest of her was covered.

His blood fizzed as if filled with champagne, his belly tightened as want swamped him. More than want. He felt—

Sayid dragged his mind back to his purpose. He

strode to the lounge chairs clustered near the window and gestured for her to take one. 'We need to talk. About marriage.'

Instantly she paled. Then predictably her jaw set. 'There's nothing to be said.'

Sayid lowered himself into a chair, resting his arms along the upholstered arms and leaning back, ostensibly at ease despite the thunder of his pulse. He refused to let her intransigence unsettle him.

'You haven't given me a reason. I deserve an explanation.'

As he watched she swiped her bottom lip with her tongue and moved to one of the other chairs. Not to sit, but to grab it with one white-knuckled hand.

Her distress made him feel wrong inside. But he was trying to do right by her! Surveying her, his indignation drained away, replaced by concern. How did she do that to him?

'Tell me, Lina.'

She stood, head bowing between her shoulders as if the weight of the world pushed down on her. Finally she stood straighter, her eyes locking with his.

'You set me free,' she said at last. 'You gave me the right to choose a future for myself.' With each word her whispering voice strengthened. 'I came to you convinced I had no choice, that I must do whatever you demanded.'

Nausea blasted him, bile rising to his tongue. 'You're saying you had sex with me because you felt compelled?' Sayid was on his feet, drenched in sweat. His skin crawled as if bitten by a million voracious desert ants.

'No, no!' Her dark hair cascaded around her as

she shook her head. 'I'm talking about before, when I first came to the palace.' She clasped her hands before her. 'I don't think you understand what your generosity did for me, Sayid. You freed me, made me feel whole. You gave me respect and *hope*.' She shrugged. 'As for our…for sex. I chose to accept your suggestion because—' again her pink tongue slicked her lip '—because I wanted to.'

Sayid frowned. There was a note in her voice that nagged. Didn't she want him any more? It was impossible that he was tortured by her absence from his bed while she felt nothing.

'You were happy with me.' And it hadn't just been the sex, he was sure of it. 'Yet you say you don't want to be my wife.' He stiffened. 'Why?'

For a second longer she held his stare, then her gaze slid away. He sensed she hid something, but what?

When she finally spoke, Lina pretended an interest in the courtyard beyond. 'You don't really want to marry me, Sayid. You simply feel obliged. But obligation isn't the way to happiness.'

He scowled. 'You refuse me because I want to protect you?' It made no sense. 'I offer you my name, my wealth, my protection and that's not *enough*?'

Lina heard his razor-sharp disbelief and forced herself to stand steady. Even now the temptation to weaken and accept him was strong.

'No, it's not enough.' She stared into his glittering gaze and threw caution to the wind. Sayid would give her no peace till she told him the truth, or at least part of it.

'You helped me believe in myself. To see that I

could shape my life the way I wanted. That I had a right to self-determination. And I've decided I want… more from marriage.'

'More than *me*?' He looked so incredulous Lina would have laughed if her heart weren't stretched to breaking point.

Sayid was right. He was so patently the stuff of feminine dreams. Caring, generous, honourable, passionate and handsome. He made problems disappear. He had money and power and…

She *had* to say no because she loved him. Because such an unequal relationship could lead only to misery.

Her fingers knotted together. 'I want a man who wants me for myself. I want love, Sayid.'

His eyes bulged, then narrowed on her as if seeing her for the first time.

'I know that's not how royal marriages are arranged. Even in my own family weddings aren't necessarily about…caring.' She swallowed hard. 'But I want more than a protector or provider. I don't want to be always indebted to my husband for saving me. I don't want to feel grateful because he deigned to choose me despite our hugely different social standings. I've seen what that did to my mother. It would destroy my self-respect.'

Even though she craved Sayid with every cell in her body.

Sayid stalked to the window, his back turned. 'Clearly that's more important to you than I am.'

'I…care for you, Sayid.'

He whipped around, his face tight. The high thrust of his cheekbones and the proud angle of his nose seemed more severely sculpted than she remembered.

'You have a strange way of showing it.'

How dared he?

How *dared* he? She was trying to explain but it was like addressing the desert wind, biting and unforgiving.

'You think I should just agree with everything you say and do? You think that's true caring?' She sucked oxygen into her starved lungs and wrapped her arms around herself, trying to hold in the pain spilling from her heart.

'I care, Sayid. I began caring for you when you were so kind to me. When you left me unmolested, and when you gave me the precious gift of an education.'

The tightness bracketing his mouth eased and his eyes softened.

'I cared even though you never expressed any pride in me or what I'd done. When I—'

The downward slice of his hand through the air cut off her words. 'You thought I wasn't proud of you?' He shook his head, looking stunned. 'But I invited you to represent the palace in that community engagement job! I invited you to attend royal events. I—'

'You never said anything to me.'

Sayid looked astounded as if she'd just tugged the fine silk carpet out from beneath his feet. Finally he spoke. 'Then let me say now that I have nothing but admiration for your achievements, Lina. Few people could have adapted and succeeded the way you did.' Sincerity throbbed in every syllable and it was like balm to her wounded soul.

'Thank you.'

But it wasn't his approval she wanted.

'I cared for you enough to take you as my lover,'

she said. Though it had been Sayid doing the taking, the sharing and demonstrating, initiating her to pleasure.

'I cared for you even more when I saw how hard you work for your people and how seriously you take your responsibilities.' She looked him full in the face. 'And I still care, even though lately you've acted like a toddler having a tantrum, throwing your weight around because you can't get your own way.'

At the look in his eyes the room seemed to darken, the air thick with a dangerous tension. He prowled across the space between them, eyes snapping in fury.

'A...tantrum?' His voice was a whisper, yet it made each hair on her neck stand on end.

'Exactly like that. Telling me I didn't have permission to leave your exalted presence. Using your position as a trump card because I wouldn't do your bidding.' His stare told her she was on perilous ground. The temper in his brilliant eyes reminded her that beneath his usually calm demeanour, Sayid was a man of strong impulses and profound feelings. And his word was law in Halarq.

She tilted her chin higher, trembling in her defiance. 'I thought you admired people who spoke the truth instead of agreeing all the time. Toadies, you called them.'

'That's different. This is about us.'

'There *is* no us.' That sliced at her fragile composure. 'We were lovers but that ended. You chose to end it. Now you want to bully me into marriage because you believe it will save my reputation.'

Lina's hands slid to her hips. 'I don't care what the gossips say about me. I'm content with my decisions.

I lived too many years tiptoeing around the sensibilities of others, not even enjoying music because it might be frowned on. Not going to school because of the outdated views of my father. Compelled to become a slave girl because that's all my family thought me good for.'

She spun away, stalked across the room then strode back, the adrenaline spike in her blood making it impossible to stand still.

'I've got news for you, Sayid. I can withstand gossip from people who mean nothing to me. But I couldn't survive being tied to a man who sees me as a duty. Or a subject to be ordered into obedience.' His head reared back but she didn't pause. 'A man who'd resent me eventually because he wasn't marrying me out of love or caring.'

Sayid's eyes blazed with a feral light that might have scared her if she had anything left to lose. But she'd faced the worst. She had to walk away from the man she loved. What else could hurt her nearly as much?

'I want more,' she said finally, her shoulders slumping as the rush of energy bled away. 'I believe I have the right to try to find happiness.' Her nails bit into her palms as she made herself continue. 'I refuse to be treated as a commodity or a problem. I have more self-respect than that.'

What about *his* self-respect?

He'd offered marriage, the most honourable offer he could make, and she'd spurned him.

Sayid was torn, proud of the woman who stood before him, refusing to be browbeaten, and at the same time horrified that she expected *love*.

He'd told himself Lina was a pragmatist. It was one of the things he admired about her. Yet it seemed she was a secret romantic.

Words crowded his tongue. Crazy, impossible words about him wanting her to stay. Needing her to, because he couldn't imagine letting her walk away.

He wanted to imprison her here in his apartments. Keep her under lock and key till she promised to stay.

Except she was right. She'd been denied self-determination before. He couldn't do that to her again.

No matter how much he needed her. For, he realised with a sudden clarity that almost cut him off at the knees, he couldn't imagine not having her with him.

Sayid flexed his hands, repressing the urge to cuff his fingers around her slender wrists and pull her close. To convince her with his mouth and body that she needed him.

'I'll see out my work with the liaison unit then I'll look for work.' Her vivid eyes fixed not on him but on something past his shoulder. 'I'm going to save up and train to be an interpreter. Senhor Neves has even talked about sponsoring me.'

Sayid ground his teeth rather than give voice to an insult about what Senhor Neves could do with his offer. Sayid's blood boiled. He was tempted to eject the man from the country, he and his whole mining team.

Except that would be unreasonable. The sort of thing his uncle would have done when crossed. Or the wild behaviour of a grown man acting like a toddler having a tantrum.

Lead plummeted through his chest to slam into his gut.

She was right. All these years proving himself
stronger than his base impulses, all these years learning moderation, yet suddenly here he was, behaving
abominably because he'd been crossed. Behaving in
ways he hadn't thought possible.

Lina had seen the worst of him. No wonder she
wanted nothing more to do with him.

'There's no need.'

Her gaze swung to his and he felt the impact as a
judder that vibrated from his chest right down to the
soles of his feet.

'Consider your debt paid.' The words ground from
a throat coated in shards of broken glass. 'You're free
to leave the palace.'

CHAPTER FOURTEEN

SAYID DIDN'T REMEMBER leaving her room, or crossing the lush courtyard.

He had no recollection of entering his own quarters.

Yet he found himself gripping the carved marble balustrade of his private balcony with nerveless hands. Before him spread the capital, a sprawl of ancient and modern. Even at this early hour it bustled with life. And beyond it the wide plain that eventually became desert.

Sayid wished he were out there now, alone in the dunes, far from everything that reminded him of Lina.

Except even in the desert there'd be no escape. Hadn't he wanted to take her there? Share that idyllic desert oasis and show her the stars?

In the other direction was the community centre they'd visited together and the old souk. On the edge of the city the spot where she'd danced at the wedding and he, like an ardent young beau, wanting to show off for his girl, had thrown himself into riding and archery contests, wanting to make her proud.

He bowed his head, feeling the sun's heat on his hands and head. Even that reminded him of Lina. The glow of warmth he felt, not just when they made love, but when she smiled at him, when she teased him and looked at him with such tenderness he'd felt…

Sayid's heart gave an almighty thump then leapt to a quicker beat. His sluggish brain fought to work its way past self-pity and regret.

Lina had looked at him so tenderly but he'd never let himself question what that meant.

Just as he'd never permitted himself to examine his own feelings beyond pride, pleasure and satisfaction.

All these years he'd worked to emulate his father rather than his uncle, focusing on moderation and honour above all things.

Yet none of those things featured in the way he'd treated Lina. Except, perhaps initially, when he'd had the strength to send her away, because he didn't trust himself not to pursue her.

And when she'd returned…

He'd told himself there was no harm in his actions, but the fact was everything he'd done had been about self-interest.

Because he wanted Lina, had always wanted her, and if the desolation engulfing him was any indication, always would.

He'd been so caught up in himself he'd forgotten about the other, huge difference between his father and his uncle. It wasn't just a matter of control or honour.

His uncle had been incapable of caring for anyone but himself. But Sayid's father had been different. He'd been a proud, strong warrior, a man's man and a born leader. Yet he had something else too. A loving heart. He'd loved Sayid's mother with an unswerving devotion that had shone like the sun. And she'd returned his feelings. No one had been surprised when she hadn't outlived him long.

Sayid forced air into his cramped lungs.

He stood still, remembering the way Lina looked at him, the warmth in her eyes. Even today as she'd blazed defiance at him there'd been something else. Something other than disappointment at his churlish ways.

She cared for him, she'd said.

Now, for the first time, Sayid let himself think about that. More, he stripped away the hard layers of protection encasing his own feelings. He forced himself to think about emotions.

It was unfamiliar and daunting. It took more courage than anything he'd done.

Yet something inside told him he'd be a coward if he didn't face this. He'd be on the slippery slope to becoming a man as flawed as his uncle. A man who'd roar his displeasure at the woman who meant everything to him. Who'd use his position to make her yield and submit. A man no woman could continue to care about.

There was a sharp hiss of air as he sucked in a breath. A blast of enlightenment, like a shaft of blue light thundering to the ground in an electrical storm.

Sayid reeled back, only his death-like grip on the stone coping saving him from falling.

Illumination spilled through him. Self-awareness. For, he saw now, he'd spent too long hiding from his feelings, pretending they didn't exist.

Yet they did. They were so deep, so broad, so all-encompassing he wondered how he'd managed to pretend they weren't there.

He shook with a palsy that stemmed from the most profound fear he'd ever known.

A fear that he'd hounded Lina into despising him. Into no longer caring for him.

He sprang back from the railing, adrenaline pulsing in his blood like the gush of oil from a desert well. His brain went into hyper-drive. Words wouldn't be enough to undo the damage he'd done. It would probably take years to get her to trust him, if she let him get close enough to try. Yet he had to convince her of his feelings.

Sayid shook his head as he strode back through his chambers.

Suddenly negotiating a peace deal with the Sheikh of Jeirut seemed simple. It was child's play compared with what he faced.

Doubt battered him. Not doubt about his feelings, but about his chances of success.

Terror wedged like a knife below his ribs, making it hard to breathe. But Sayid forced himself on. He couldn't give up, simply because he couldn't imagine his world without Lina in it.

Lina kept her head up as she walked through the wide reception hall with its double storey pillars and vast gilded ceiling.

The chamberlain had assured her the bag she'd hastily packed would be delivered to the taxi she'd ordered. For a moment she'd been tempted to sneak out the back entrance, the servants' entrance where she'd first arrived all those years ago, so she didn't meet anyone she knew. But pride demanded she exit through the main doors. Besides, she'd promised herself she'd look in on Makram in his office on her way out.

Not, she assured herself, for a possible last glimpse of Sayid. Just to thank Makram for his kindness and friendship.

Lina bit her lip and continued on her way, trying to distract her thoughts by concentrating on the magnificence surrounding her, rather than the raw pain pulsing inside.

Halfway across the echoing space she became aware of footsteps behind her. Steady yet quick, they came closer and closer. Her nape prickled and she swallowed hard.

It was *not* Sayid. Her mind played tricks. If Sayid saw her he'd pivot on his heel and walk away. The things she'd said to him—

'Lina!'

A jolt of fire ripped through her, turning her lungs to an inferno and searing through her efforts at composure. She blinked back the sudden, terrible glaze of heat behind her eyes and kept walking, her pace faltering but persistent.

In the distance she saw a couple of Sayid's advisers, absorbed in discussion, cross the doorway that led to the audience chamber. A woman, one of the education advisers, passed into another corridor leading to the royal offices.

This was too public a place to face Sayid.

A bubble of desperate laughter rose in her parched throat. It didn't matter where she was, she couldn't talk to him. Not when misery and grief filled her.

Her heart ached. Her whole body—

'Lina. Please!' He was right behind her and there

was something in his voice that made her stumble to a halt. She told herself her own desperation had made her imagine it. It wasn't possible Sayid felt like that.

Yet now she'd stopped she couldn't seem to start again. Even though she felt the warmth of his tall frame at her back and heard his breathing above her ear. He was too close! She'd never be able to conceal her feelings.

'Aren't you going to look at me?' His voice was deep and soft. The suede voice she remembering from lovemaking and from midnight chats as she lay curled in his arms.

Fiercely she blinked, fighting back welling emotion. It wasn't fair. *He* wasn't fair! Using that voice when he knew it made her melt.

Since when has life been fair, Lina?

'Please?'

It was a breath of air drifting over her scalp, sending trickles of awareness down her nape and spine, drawing her belly tight and making her nipples pucker.

She was so weak around Sayid. She'd tried to be strong for such a long time but now her resolve turned to water.

With a sigh and a silent prayer, she turned.

The man before her stole her breath.

For once it wasn't because of that jolt of attraction, the awareness of his charismatic good looks. It was his expression that stunned her. Even his posture was different. Not arrogantly or even tenderly confident.

Sayid looked…lost. His features drawn. The tension in his big frame vibrated into the air around him. His mouth was a flat line, not with ire, but something that looked like nerves. And his eyes!

Lina swayed towards him, drawn by the look in his eyes. It was only when he grabbed her elbows and a new kind of heat washed through her that she realised how close she'd moved.

She tried to step back but his hands were rock-hard.

'No. Please.' Lina frowned. Even his voice sounded different. 'We must talk.'

Common sense told her to walk away because talking with Sayid would only give her time to weaken. Instead she found herself saying, 'Not here. It's too public.'

They were in the palace, but right at the heart of the public rooms. People passing couldn't hear what they said, but they were in full view of any passers-by.

Sayid's mouth quirked up at one side in a parody of a smile. Even that sent a pang through her chest. 'That's exactly why it has to be here.'

'I don't understand.' Lina told herself that didn't matter. She owed it to herself to get away before he used her feelings for him to bend her to his will, yet she couldn't summon the energy to move.

'You deserve more than a secret affair, Lina, as if you're not good enough to be acknowledged publicly.'

His words struck at the core of icy hurt lodged inside her, yet she couldn't let that matter. 'I know you want to do the right thing by me publicly. But marriage—'

'No! That's not what I want.'

Lina frowned. He didn't want to marry her any more? Of course he didn't. She'd rejected him and insulted him to boot. A proud man like Sayid wouldn't come back for more.

'I proposed…' Again that stark parody of a smile.

'No, I didn't even have the decency to propose, did I?'
He hefted a deep breath but it didn't still the tremor
she felt in his large hands.

Suddenly Lina felt not only out of her depth but
scared. She'd never seen Sayid like this, so drawn
and vulnerable. Of their own volition her hands went
to his chest, curling into the fine weave of his suit.
Beneath her right hand his heart sprinted like her
own.

'Sayid, what is it?' She shouldn't care yet she did.
Her love for him wasn't a tap she could turn off at
will.

'I don't deserve your concern, Lina. Not yet at
least.' He lifted one hand to her face, tracing from
her cheek down to her jaw and lingering at her throat,
making waves of desire curl and crest within her.

'I said marriage between us would protect you.
That my concern was for your reputation. And that
was true, as far as it went.'

Beneath her hand Lina felt his chest rise on a
mighty breath. 'But still I lied.'

Her eyes widened and he nodded. 'I'm not proud
of it. I'm not proud of the way I've treated you. You
were right—I behaved as if you were a toy someone
had snatched away. As if I had a *right* to you.'

His hand came to rest on her shoulder, his fingers
kneading gently. 'No one has that right, Lina.'

She nodded, feeling the weight of his words and at
the same time experiencing a lightening inside where
pain resided. It meant so much that he understood.

'But how did you lie to me?'

She watched his expression cloud with something
that almost looked like fear. 'I lied by letting you think

I was driven by concern for your reputation. At the time I believed it. Well—' he shrugged '—by that and lust.' Fire simmered in the look he sent her and she felt the burn right to her toes.

'What I didn't tell you, what I didn't acknowledge to myself, was that I cared about you, Lina, not as a mistress or a ward. Not as a responsibility.' He paused and she heard him swallow. 'But as the only woman I've ever loved.'

Lina stared up into his proud face, seeing for the first time the truth in those dark eyes that so often before had been unreadable.

Shock slammed into her and she staggered, only Sayid's hold keeping her upright.

'Lina? Lina! Are you all right?'

All right? When the man she'd adored since she was seventeen said he loved her?

'Do you mean it?' She wanted so much to believe but it was too incredible.

'More than anything, sweet Lina.' This time his half-smile held the smoky promise that always made her toes curl. 'You're the sun and the stars to me, *habib albi*. You are my heart and my soul. You make me want to be a better man.'

Emotion clotted in Lina's throat as she read the truth in his eyes. She barely had time to register it before he was bending, slipping down onto his knees before her.

'Sayid?' She looked into his face and saw nothing but joy and fierce determination. 'What are you doing?'

'Proving as best I can that I love you. That whatever society says, I will never, can never be superior to you. You're stronger and better than me in so many ways. Besides—' he paused, a smile kinking the corner of his mouth '—I believe this is the customary pose for a man proposing marriage to the woman he loves.'

The woman he loves. Lina told herself it wasn't possible, yet truth resonated in his words. It was there in his expression, and his fierce grip on her hands.

Over his head she caught movement. On the far side of the huge chamber a courtier stopped to stare. Then two more figures emerged and came to a halt, their faces turning towards Sayid and Lina.

'But you're the supreme ruler. You can't do this here. People will see and talk and—'

'Let them. I'm a man before I'm the Emir and I'm proud of my feelings for you. I love you, Lina. I want you to marry me because I love you and I'm hoping that perhaps you care for me enough to agree.'

A thrill coursed through her. Sayid loved her, genuinely loved her.

His fingers tightened on hers. 'Have you nothing to say?' It wasn't a demand but a plea and Lina's heart rolled over.

'Get up first.'

'But I—'

'Please, Sayid. I don't want you on your knees before me. I want us to be equals.'

He rose, hands sliding to her elbows, drawing her in. 'And are we?' There was such tension in him as he waited for her reply, for a moment it stole her voice.

Silently she nodded. 'I've loved you since I was seventeen. I can't stop now, no matter how I try.'

Strong arms curved around her. 'I don't want you

to stop. Ever. I want you as my lover, my partner, my wife, always.'

He released one of her hands and reached into his pocket. Then he withdrew a fistful of gleaming pearls, huge and, she guessed, priceless. He lifted his hand, offering it to her. Lina realised he held a double string of pearls, a necklace with a faceted pendant of rich amethyst.

Her breath caught. 'From the royal treasury?' She'd heard of its fabled wealth.

'The pendant is. I went there looking for something specifically for you. This was the closest I came to matching your beautiful eyes. But the pearls aren't royal treasure.'

'They look it.' She lifted her gaze to his face, seeing her own wonder and excitement mirrored there.

'These mean far more. They aren't booty from some ancient war, or a present designed to flatter and appease a powerful sheikh. They were the betrothal gift my father gave my mother. They are a symbol of love, gratitude and fidelity.'

Lina's throat worked at the timbre of his voice, the hope and uncertainty that feathered across her skin.

'Will you accept me as your one true love? For that's what you are to me—the only woman I'll ever love. The only woman I could possibly share my life with.'

Lina's vision misted but it didn't stop her smiling as she looked up into his eyes. 'I will, my heart. Always.'

Then Sayid, with a complete disregard for royal protocol, did something that had never before been done in that echoing, magnificent room. He lifted her in his arms and swung her round and round with a shout of triumph and jubilation.

Then he lowered her gently to her feet and kissed her with all the tenderness and love a woman could desire.

* * * * *

If you enjoyed
INHERITED FOR THE ROYAL BED
why not explore these other stories
by Annie West?

CONTRACTED FOR THE PETRAKIS HEIR
HIS MAJESTY'S TEMPORARY BRIDE
THE GREEK'S FORBIDDEN PRINCESS
THE DESERT KING'S CAPTIVE BRIDE

Available now!

#3645 THE ITALIAN'S ONE-NIGHT CONSEQUENCE
One Night With Consequences
by Cathy Williams

When Leo meets Maddie, their irresistible chemistry ignites. Then Leo learns Maddie is heiress to the company he wants—and she's *pregnant*! To secure his heir, can Leo strike a deal to meet Maddie at the altar?

#3646 TYCOON'S RING OF CONVENIENCE
by Julia James

Socialite Diana's determination to save her family home provides self-made billionaire Nikos with the opportunity to propose a temporary marriage. But during their honeymoon, Nikos awakens Diana's simmering desire! Now Nikos craves more from his not-so-convenient wife...

#3647 BOUND BY THE BILLIONAIRE'S VOWS
by Clare Connelly

When Skye learns her marriage to Matteo is built on lies, she demands a divorce. But Matteo isn't willing to let Skye go so easily—the price of her freedom is one last night together!

#3648 A CINDERELLA FOR THE DESERT KING
by Kim Lawrence

When shy Abby pledges herself to a mysterious stranger, she's shocked to learn he's heir to the throne. Swept into Zain's world of exquisite pleasure, can this innocent Cinderella ever become this powerful sheikh's queen?

HPCNM0718RB

Get 4 FREE REWARDS!

We'll send you 2 FREE Books plus 2 FREE Mystery Gifts.

Harlequin Presents® books feature a sensational and sophisticated world of international romance where sinfully tempting heroes ignite passion.

FREE
Value Over
$20

YES! Please send me 2 FREE Harlequin Presents® novels and my 2 FREE gifts (gifts are worth about $10 retail). After receiving them, if I don't wish to receive any more books, I can return the shipping statement marked "cancel." If I don't cancel, I will receive 6 brand-new novels every month and be billed just $4.55 each for the regular-print edition or $5.55 each for the larger-print edition in the U.S., or $5.49 each for the regular-print edition or $5.99 each for the larger-print edition in Canada. That's a savings of at least 11% off the cover price! It's quite a bargain! Shipping and handling is just 50¢ per book in the U.S. and 75¢ per book in Canada*. I understand that accepting the 2 free books and gifts places me under no obligation to buy anything. I can always return a shipment and cancel at any time. The free books and gifts are mine to keep no matter what I decide.

Choose one: ☐ **Harlequin Presents®**
Regular-Print
(106/306 HDN GMYX)

☐ **Harlequin Presents®**
Larger-Print
(176/376 HDN GMYX)

Name (please print)

Address   Apt. #

City   State/Province   Zip/Postal Code

Mail to the **Reader Service:**
IN U.S.A.: P.O. Box 1341, Buffalo, NY 14240-8531
IN CANADA: P.O. Box 603, Fort Erie, Ontario L2A 5X3

Want to try two free books from another series? Call 1-800-873-8635 or visit www.ReaderService.com.

"You want me to move?"

"Yes."

A gleam pulsed in his eyes. "Make me."

Instead of closing her hand into a fist and aiming it at
his nose as he deserved, Chloe placed it flat on his cheek.

An unwitting sigh escaped from her lips as she drank
in the ruggedly handsome features she had dreamed
about for so long. The texture of his skin was so different
from her own, smooth but with the bristles of his stubble
breaking through...had he not shaved? She had never
seen his face anything other than clean-shaven.

He was close enough for her to catch the faint trace of
coffee and the more potent scent of his cologne.

Luis was the cause of all this chaos rampaging through
her. She hated him so much, but the feelings she'd carried
for him for all these years were still there, refusing to die,

Coming next month, a tale of inescapable passion!

**In *THE GREEK'S BOUGHT BRIDE*
by Sharon Kendrick!**

Tamsyn is about to get a shocking proposal from devastating Greek billionaire Xan. But will she accept his convenient ring?

Tamsyn lost her innocence in a spectacularly sensual night with a Greek billionaire. She didn't expect to see notorious playboy Xan again, until he proposes a marriage of convenience! It's hard to refuse when he's promising incredible wealth and her pregnant sister desperately needs support, but Xan is dangerously addictive… If Tamsyn isn't careful, she could lose herself to the Greek—for good!

The Greek's Bought Bride
part of the **Conveniently Wed!** miniseries!

Available August 2018

making her doubt herself and what she'd believed to be
the truth.

Her lips tingled, yearning to feel his mouth on
hers again, all her senses springing to life and waving
surrender flags at her.

Just kiss him ...

Closing her eyes tightly, Chloe gathered all her wits
about her, wriggled out from under him and sat up.

Her lungs didn't want to work properly, and she had to
force air into them.

She shifted to the side, needing physical distance,
suddenly terrified of what would happen if she were to
brush against him or touch him in any form again.

Fighting to clear her head of the fog clouding it, she
blinked rapidly and said, "Do I have your word that your
feud with Benjamin ends with our marriage?"

Things had gone far enough. It was time to put an end
to it.

"*Sí*. Marry me and it ends."

Don't miss
MARRIAGE MADE IN BLACKMAIL,
available August 2018,
and the first part of Michelle Smart's
RINGS OF VENGEANCE trilogy
BILLIONAIRE'S BRIDE FOR REVENGE,
available now wherever Harlequin Presents® books
and ebooks are sold.

www.Harlequin.com